ALSO BY

MARCO MALVALDI

Game for Five

THREE-CARD MONTE

Marco Malvaldi

THREE-CARD MONTE

*Translated from the Italian
by Howard Curtis*

Europa
editions

Europa Editions
214 West 29th Street
New York, N.Y. 10001
www.europaeditions.com
info@europaeditions.com

Copyright © 2008 by Sellerio editore, Palermo
First Publication 2014 by Europa Editions

Translation by Howard Curtis
Original title: *Il gioco delle tre carte*
Translation copyright © 2014 by Europa Editions

Library of Congress Cataloging in Publication Data is available
ISBN 978-1-60945-205-6

Malvaldi, Marco
Three-Card Monte

Book design and cover illustration by Emanuele Ragnisco
www.mekkanografici.com

Prepress by Grafica Punto Print – Rome

Printed in the USA

To Vittorio,
who in going into the light
has left us a little more in the dark

Who steals my purse steals trash; 'tis something, nothing;
'Twas mine, 'tis his, and has been slave to thousands;
But he that filches from me my good name
Robs me of that which not enriches him,
And makes me poor indeed.
WILLIAM SHAKESPEARE—*Othello*, Act III, Scene III

THREE-CARD MONTE

If this was chaos, then Italy must be the most beautiful country in the world. That was what Koichi Kawaguchi thought soon after getting off Flight JL3476, which had picked him up at Narita Airport in Tokyo and brought him down, amid incomprehensible applause from the Italians on the plane, on one of the runways of Fiumicino Airport in Rome.

Koichi Kawaguchi had been apprehensive. This was the first time he had ever left Japan, not just to go to a conference, but in general, and he had heard that Italy was a beautiful but extremely chaotic and disorganized country. Moreover, Koichi was an almost pathologically nervous person. So the idea of being alone in an unknown airport, in a country where he did not speak the language, having to take a domestic flight that left just two hours after he landed from Tokyo, had been making him feel anxious for the past month.

But in fact things had gone better than expected.

To start with, as he left Narita he had recognized a few people who were going to the conference. Even though he did not know them personally, Koichi had seen a number of young men carrying, along with their other baggage, cylindrical plastic tubes, which identified them immediately as people going to a scientific conference.

At a conference, the younger delegates rarely talk or deliver papers. What they usually have is a so-called "poster session": a short period of time in which every young would-be scientist explains personally, in a very informal way, to any delegate who stops in front of his poster what kind of research he has been working on. The poster in question is usually kept, carefully rolled, inside one of these aforementioned cylindrical tubes, which do not usually pass unnoticed—not, incidentally, because of their elegant design, but rather thanks to their perverse functionality: these contraptions seem to have been expressly designed for the purpose of getting caught in any opening that presents itself, such as between the legs of the inexperienced owner and his nearest neighbors. This unpredictable dynamic often leads to lots of tripping up, near-falls, and involuntary bag snatching, thus rather spectacularly breaking the monotony of the terminal.

Beyond their troublesome consequences at the mechanical level, the tubes had allowed Koichi to recognize potential conference delegates, and from the conversations of which he had caught snatches he had realized that they were going to the same conference.

That was why he had decided, with a typically Japanese mixture of shyness and resolution, not to lose sight of the group of compatriots and to follow them discreetly, but without introducing himself. It was his first journey abroad, and he wanted to savor it as much as possible by himself. In spite of that, he was quite determined to shadow his countrymen and to use them as guide dogs, especially on arriving at Fiumicino where, he was convinced, he would find himself facing a state of chaos worthy of Dante.

Instead of which, he had found the Roman airport surprisingly calm. No trace of that overflowing flood of yelling people, infiltrated by hordes of pickpockets greedy for wallets from the Land of the Rising Sun, which had characterized his waking nightmares for some weeks. No screaming, no clamor, in fact a surprisingly small number of people. Compared with the crowds at Shinjuku station on the Tokyo subway, into which he descended every morning, this was like the members of a soccer team spread out across the field compared with the people on the terraces.

His first impression of the airport was quite disappointing. It seemed a tad provincial: the few shops on the upper floor were ugly, and the restaurant-pizzeria-cafeteria and the two bars that competed with each other to feed the newly-landed traveler were not at all inviting.

And yet, unexpectedly, he liked the place.

He liked the apparent calm with which the Italians did things, the smile with which the police officer had checked his passport and wished him a pleasant stay—in surprisingly halting English for someone who worked in an airport. The inexplicable yet obvious satisfaction of the barman from whom he ordered a coffee, as if having a coffee at that hour and in that bar was the right thing to do for someone who knew the ways of the world. And the coffee, dark and concentrated, served in an already warmed-up cup, was very good.

There were other things he liked less, like the toilets. He had heard that the Italians were the cleanest people in Europe. Clearly, he had found himself thinking, the toilets at the airport must have been conceived for Germans. Spacious, certainly, but with incredibly wet and dirty floors, and a faucet that, if you turned it less than halfway, let out a wretched little drop every two or three seconds, or else, if you turned it more than halfway, was like opening the floodgates on a dam. And on top of that, the toilet seat, unlike that coffee cup, was not warmed up. In all public toilets in Tokyo, the toilet seats were warmed up. Obviously the Italians and the Japanese had different ideas about what needed to be warmed up.

Proceeding to the check-in hall, Koichi saw that the plane that should have been leaving just two hours after the flight from Tokyo had landed was comfortably delayed by two hours.

This calmed him further. In fact, it calmed him so much

that he decided, fully in tune with the Italian spirit now, to go back to the bar and have another coffee.

"Coffee, please. What would you like?"

"A coffee for me too."

"An orange juice for me. If I have another coffee I'll be climbing up the walls."

That morning, when the barman at Galilei airport in Pisa had seen the three young men for the first time, they had definitely looked better. Now, at five in the evening, after waiting for seven hours in the airport's only terminal, they looked a little stricken. Their shirts, in spite of constant tucking in, stuck out asymmetrically from their pants, and one of the three had vast rings of sweat beneath their armpits. Their faces were haggard, and their desultory conversation consisted of grunts and generalized moaning.

"Anyway, this is the last time I let them fuck me over like this."

"Of course it is. You said the same thing last year. And this is bound to be the last time we let them fuck us over like this anyway. I don't know about you two, but there's no way they're going to renew my grant."

The man talking this way was the oldest of the three young men—if you can call someone of about thirty old—a tall, broad-shouldered fellow, with well-defined features and a number of earrings in his right earlobe. The grant he was referring to was the 238.56 euros a month for a year that he had been generously awarded the previous year by the Department of Chemistry and Industrial Chemistry in Pisa, after obtaining his doctorate, to tide him over until—as his professor had said to him—"things improve and we can find you something a little more permanent," or alternatively—as he himself put it— "one of those old codgers who pretend to be worried about us realizes that he's a hundred years old, retires to the country to grow turnips, and frees up a place, dammit."

The two other young men, though, were still studying for their doctorates, and the position of all three, as always in the case of academics without tenure, involved unwritten burdens it was unthinkable to shirk. One of these was that if your department happened to organize a conference you had to be part, unofficially but compulsorily, of the organizing committee. What this meant, practically speaking, was that you had to attend to the needs of the external delegates arriving for the conference.

That was why, on the occasion of the Twelfth International Workshop on Macromolecular and Biomacromolecular Chemistry, the three of them had been conscripted by the secretary of the Department of Chemistry to fetch the various groups of foreign professors and students from the airport and escort them to their hotel. Having welcomed austere Scandinavian academics, heaved the trunks of elderly American female scholars, tracked down the lost baggage and children of hysterical Spanish researchers, also female, and guided herds of Japanese scientists to the capacious bus that would take them to the hotel, they were now almost at the end of their labors. There was only one person still to come, and he should be arriving on the last flight, after which the three of them would be free to go home. As often happens when a thankless task is nearing completion, they were all at the end of their tether.

"Well, let's hope this Dutch guy gets here soon," said one of the other two, trying to put aside the matter of the grant, which would only have led to unpleasantness between them. In the course of the day, they had in fact talked a lot about their situation as academics without tenure. The conclusion they had reached was basically this: that researchers without tenure were regarded by the university and the Ministry as being pretty much like intestinal flora—in other words, parasites. Good parasites, necessary for the proper functioning of the organism (since they were the ones actually doing all the work in the labs), but kept alive on the residue of those resources that had been ingested and, in the last analysis, stuck in a situation that could objectively be described as crap.

"Does anyone know this Snijders?" asked the third. "We aren't going to have to run all over the airport after him like that Hungarian, are we?"

"No, no," the tall young man said. "I know him, I've seen him before at a couple of conferences. You can't mistake him."

"How come?"

"You'll see soon enough."

"You'll see right now," said the third with a smile. "Look, they've arrived. I can see movement."

"Great! Let's go get the Kraut, and then we can go home."

"He's Dutch."

"Dutch or Swedish, who cares as long as he's the last of them?"

Once they had reached the terminal, the tall young man raised above his head a sign with the words *Twelfth International Workshop on Macromolecular and Biomacromolecular Chemistry* written on it (by hand: you use the means at your disposal). Almost immediately, a man of about forty-five detached himself from the group of people coming out of the terminal. He was some way short of six feet tall and wore a khaki K-Way that gave particular prominence to the orange T-shirt under it, inserted as best it could be into a remarkably creased pair of beltless jeans that ended four inches above his calves, which in turn emerged from a pair of hi-tech trekking sandals. The man, who seemed to have no luggage apart from a backpack, walked up to them and raised a hand in greeting.

"Hello, Professor Snijders," the tall young man said in Italian. "Did you have a good trip?"

"Oh, yes, a very good trip," the man replied, also in Italian but with a strange and very marked accent.

Antonius Celsius Jacopus Snijders (Anton to his friends, which included a large number of people) didn't look like someone who worked as a professor. To tell the truth, he didn't like someone who worked at all, or had ever worked a day in his life. In reality, however odd he might look from the outside, Anton Snijders was an excellent lecturer and a good researcher, able to manage a team of some ten other researchers in a dignified and original way.

"You speak Italian?" said one of the two graduate students, asking a clearly pointless question out of pure politeness.

"My wife is Italian," Snijders replied with great practicality to what he supposed—correctly—was the genuine question, that is, "Why do you speak Italian?" That was something about the Italians that never failed to intrigue him: they rarely asked direct questions. The young man found it strange that a Dutchman should speak Italian, but would have considered it impolite to ask him straight out, "Why do you speak Italian?" He himself wouldn't have worried about it—when it came to politeness, Snijders never worried too much—but they did. Strange. He focused on one of the young men, who was now giving him logistical instructions.

"The hotel is a quarter of an hour from here by taxi. We'll call you one immediately."

"No, thanks. There's no need."

"Do you have someone waiting for you?" one of the three asked.

"I was thinking I'd walk to the hotel."

The three looked at each other. From the expressions on their faces, it was obvious they didn't think they'd heard correctly.

"Look, Professor," said one of the three, emphasizing the word Professor, maybe to remind him that intellectuals were usually expected to be somewhat below par physically, "the hotel is six miles from here."

"I know," Snijders said, still smiling. "I've been sitting for three hours. I'd like to stretch my legs."

"Are you sure? It's six miles. It'll take two hours."

"I'm in no hurry."

The scene might make you think of a religious ritual. Which is strange, because it takes place amid the tables outside a bar.

The priest is a tall man in his thirties with a large hooked nose and a vaguely Middle Eastern air. He moves with hieratic calm between the tamarisks and the tables, his pace solemn and methodical. In his arms, he is carrying, as if it were a baby, a small laptop, which he consults with an air that wavers constantly between the pleased and the dismayed as he explores the jungle of chairs and umbrellas. He must know the place well, since he moves without looking up from the screen, but still manages to avoid upsetting the various pieces of furniture. Sometimes, at what may be thought particularly significant stations of the liturgy, he begins to make strange, vaguely cruciform signs with the computer, while his lips move in mute prayer. From a distance, only disconnected fragments of the prayer can be heard, things like, "Dammit, there was a signal only a few seconds ago."

Instead of the pious ladies who usually crowd places of worship, there is a pretty redhead in a white T-shirt with the words *Bar Lume* on it. The rest of her attire goes unnoticed, but the T-shirt remains engraved on the mind. All right, not only the T-shirt. The girl is watching the supposed priest with little faith and a great deal of anxiety, and making little crosses on a sheet of paper on which the outside of the bar has been sketchily drawn.

Not far from the priest, four strange choirboys are following his every move with a placid, relaxed air. Strange, firstly, thanks to their age, given that choirboys are usually between ten and fifteen years old, whereas the characters in question hover around their seventies. Strange, too, thanks to their language, because even though it is normal for choirboys to talk during mass, if they used the vocabulary of the old man in the beret and pullover they'd be disqualified for life. From time to time, the priest turns and glares at them, but like real choirboys they take hardly any notice of him and continue talking.

"What did you say this new bunch of crap is called?"

"Wi-fi."

"What?"

"Wi-fi, Ampelio. It means without wires. It's a way to connect to the web."

The person talking is Aldo, a handsome-looking widower in his seventies. Aldo is the only representative of the quartet of mature lads not to have yielded to the blandishments of a pension: for several years he's owned and run a restaurant called the Boccaccio. The Boccaccio boasts brusque but polite service, an extensive cellar that ranges from France to New Zealand, and an exceptional cook, Otello Brondi, familiarly known as Tavolone because of the size of his hands.

A lover of baroque music, classical literature, and women who are still breathing, Aldo is currently one of the three or four people alive able to express himself in grammatically correct Italian, absolutely devoid of Anglicisms and decidedly refined.

Something of which his direct interlocutor is proudly incapable. This person's name is Ampelio, he is eighty-three years old and is the grandfather of the barman. He has had a happy past as a stationmaster, labor organizer, and amateur cyclist, and now has a serene present of afternoons and evening, spent in the company of his elderly friends at his grandson's bar. His grandson being the man wandering about with a laptop in his hands.

"You mean it's like the Internet?"

"It *is* the Internet, but without wires. If you have a portable computer, you come to the bar and connect directly without needing any wires."

"Right, I've got it. You arrive at the bar and instead of talking to Ugo and Gino you connect to the Internet and see what's happening in Australia. While you're looking at what's happening in Australia, a few feet away Ugo and Gino are talking about how well your girlfriend fucks. Do me a favor . . . "

"Ampelio, don't talk crap. The Internet is a means to an end. It all depends on how you use it. You have access to billions of pieces of information. You know everything about everybody, things that are true and even things that are false. All at incredible speed and without leaving your own home."

"You're right, Aldo," Del Tacca says. "You know everything about everybody as soon as it happens, even when nothing happens. And without leaving home. It's just like your wife, Ampelio, but at least you can turn it off."

The third man who has spoken is known to the inhabitants of Pineta simply as "Del Tacca from the Town Hall." This is so as not to confuse him with "Del Tacca from the New Harbor," who lives next to the new harbor, "Del Tacca from the Streetcar," who used to be a ticket collector on the streetcar, and "Del Tacca from the Service Station on the Avenue," about whose activities it seems best to keep silent, let's just say he isn't a pump attendant. Del Tacca from the Town Hall is a short, fat man, almost broader than he is tall, who at first sight may seem a little aloof, but who in fact is as unpleasant as a piece of shit under your shoe. A virtue developed, along with his large proportion of adipose tissue, in the course of his years of so-called work at the town hall in Pineta: years of compulsory breakfasts, lost files, and semi-clandestine games of *tres-*

sette while a line of people waits at a counter displaying a sign that says, "I'll be right back."

In the meantime, the priest has closed the computer screen and sat down at the attractive girl's table. The girl's name is Tiziana and she's been working at the Bar Lume for two or three years as a maid of all work. The aforementioned Bar Lume is owned by Massimo, who corresponds physically to both the priest and Ampelio's grandson. In other words, the man who has sat down is called Massimo, and he's the barman.

Massimo lights a cigarette, looks at the sheet of paper Tiziana hands him, and frowns.

"That's all." It isn't a question, it's a statement. Rather a disconsolate one.

"Yes. That's all." Tiziana doesn't add anything else. She would like to speak because she is a lively, good-natured girl, as well as an intelligent person. Being intelligent, she soon grasped the fact that her employer particularly hates pointless questions and, although with a certain effort, she avoids asking them.

"So, let's go over this. The four tables near the tamarisks don't have any signal at all."

"Yes. I mean no, they don't."

"The three near the pillar, a weak signal."

"That's right."

"And the table under the elms, a full signal."

"That's right. So . . . "

So we're screwed, Massimo thinks. Shit, it isn't possible. It's a conspiracy. I equip the bar with Internet, I spend a small fortune on it, I lose what remains of my mind installing it, setting it up correctly and everything, and in the end what happens? It doesn't work. Worse still, it works in fits and starts. The signal's useless. It wavers, it fades, it spits. But in one spot, dammit, there's a signal. A strong, clear, firm signal. At one table. The table under the elm. The table where my grandfather and those other worshipers of Gerovital have been spending all afternoon every afternoon, from April to October, ever since I opened. I'm sorry, but to hell with them. I need that table.

It's afternoon, and the bar, together with most of the town, is indulging in the long postprandial nap that precedes aperitif time. The only people outside are two girls sitting next to the tamarisks over a laptop and two coffee shakeratos, and the four standard-bearers for the elderly, proudly enthroned on the chairs around the table under the elm. After taking the old-timers' orders, Tiziana comes back into the bar.

"Massimo?"

"All present and correct."

"So, two espressos, one regular for your grandpa and one with a shot of Sassolino for Aldo. An Averna with ice for Pilade and a chinotto for Rimediotti."

"Right. Make the coffees for me, Tiziana, please. I'll see to the rest."

Massimo takes a wooden tray, puts it on the counter, bends under the counter, and takes out a little bottle of dark liquid. He looks at it lovingly for a moment, then grabs it and shakes it hard for about ten seconds.

He places it delicately on the tray with the bottle opener next to it, then pours a finger of amaro into a glass, adding to it for completeness's sake another half-finger of balsamic vinegar. Then he picks up a small ice cube directly with his fingers and drops it with a professional air in the glass. Finally, he conscientiously examines the two espressos that Tiziana has made and placed on the tray. He takes a neat sip of both, then in an authoritative manner tops up the contents of the cups with sparkling water taken directly from the refrigerator, and adds a squirt of lemon juice for Aldo, who does after all want it with a shot.

"Ready, you can take them."

"Massimo, come on . . . "

"What?"

"Don't play the fool, come on."

"Never offend the boss. It's bad manners and not very clever. I could fire you, you know."

"I didn't say you are a fool, I said you play the fool. I'm sorry, but those poor old guys . . . "

"Poor old guys my ass. Did you or didn't you ask them if they could please change tables?"

"Yes, Massimo, but even you have to realize—"

"Not 'even you.' Only you. Massimo has to understand. Massimo has to understand that these poor old guys are creatures of habit. Massimo has to understand that it's cool under the elm. Plus, I don't see why Massimo has to get so upset. The bar doesn't even belong to him. The old-timers have taken it over. He should just accept the fact."

"Well, I'm not taking them these things."

"No problem. Rimediotti's coming."

Sure enough, one of the old men has entered the bar. An old man in slightly worse shape than the others. He is tall and emaciated, and is wearing a blue T-shirt with horizontal stripes and pale-colored pants, an ensemble that gives him an ambiguous air, halfway between a nursing home patient and an escaped convict.

Massimo has always heard him called "Rimediotti," and only after many years did he discover that long, long ago he had been christened Gino. He's a quiet old man, with vaguely nostalgic ideas about the Fascist period, and a notable billiard player.

"Have you done them, Massimo? Can I take them?"

"Please, Rimediotti, go ahead."

Rimediotti takes the tray and heads outside. Massimo hears the radio playing "Y.M.C.A." by the Village People, turns up the volume, and starts washing the glasses in time to the music. When he looks up, he sees through the window the four old-timers at the table gesticulating, apparently engaged in an unlikely dance to the rhythm of the gay-themed music echoing inside the bar. After a while, all four of them get resolutely to their feet, but instead of going "Why-Em-See-Eh" with their arms, as Massimo has been imagining, they troop into the bar, led by Ampelio.

They come in all talking, or rather yelling, at the same time. Through careful sifting of the acoustic signal, necessary to separate the voices of the old geezers from the cheerful howls coming from the radio, it becomes clear that Rimediotti is accusing Massimo of ruining his clothes, Aldo is accusing him of spoiling his digestion, and Ampelio is accusing him of having a whore for a mother. Only Del Tacca remains silent, and simply glares daggers at Massimo. Massimo feels compelled to ask him, "What about you, Pilade, don't you have anything to complain about?"

"Do you think that was amaro I was drinking?" Del Tacca replies, continuing to glare at him.

"You aren't normal!" cries Rimediotti, his comb-over slick with chinotto, as a result of the little bottle exploding, which makes him look even more of a disaster area. "You're a criminal! You're a moron, you are! That's what you are! An idiot! How is it possible?"

"I'm sorry, Rimediotti," says Massimo, continuing to wash the glasses. "It happens sometimes, you know that. The bottle tops explode. I think it's because of the pressure of the carbon dioxide inside. Or rather, the difference in pressure between inside and outside. Among other things. I read somewhere that the difference in pressure is greater if you're sitting under an elm. In my opinion, if you'd been sitting next to the tamarisks, nothing would have happened. Can I get you something else?" Massimo asks in his diligent barman's tone.

Massimo's proposal meets with a grim silence from the old-timers.

When two strong wills share a common objective, and neither of the two has any intention of retreating from his own position, a conflict is inevitable. Like two engine blocks, the adversaries approach each other without any concern for the consequences, and without any possibility of changing their minds. Whoever is toughest wins.

History is full of such episodes. Think, for example, of Caesar and Antony. Think of Churchill and Stalin. Think of Zidane and Materazzi.

Here, too, the Moment has arrived. We are heading for a collision. The air seems to freeze, as befits a duel, while the adversaries eye each other warily. Unfortunately, instead of the music of Morricone, which would suit it perfectly, the soundtrack to this confrontation consists of the inappropriately cheerful screeching of the Village People, who are still insisting that there is no way you can be unhappy if you're hanging out with the boys.

Heedless of this pleasant background, the duelists study each other threateningly.

Slowly but inevitably, the music fades.

The song is about to finish.

Very soon, the moment will come.

"Excuse me . . . "

It's a timid, polite voice, barely audible. But it's more than enough to break the spell. The voice belongs to one of the two girls who were outside at the table next to the tamarisks. She has come into the bar and is looking at the group with a pair of very, very large blue eyes, like those you see in Japanese cartoons. Behind her, her friend also enters. She has the expression of an innocent child combined with cleavage that's decidedly maternal. Massimo looks at the first girl in a manner at once questioning and polite, while the old-timers unconditionally approve of her friend.

"I wanted to ask you a favor. I need to use the Internet, but it isn't working very well at our table. Umm . . . . I've seen that there's a good signal at the next table, so I wanted to ask if it's possible to change tables."

This is followed by a moment of palpable embarrassment.

"Don't ask me, ask these gentlemen, it's their table," Massimo says with ill-concealed perfidy, pointing at the old-timers.

Having, with mysterious feminine wisdom, identified Ampelio as their leader, the girl looks at him and smiles. "Would you mind changing?"

She underlines the question by opening and closing her big eyes persuasively. Ampelio mutters something in embarrassment, while Rimediotti says gallantly, "Good heavens, signorina, you don't even need to ask. Please, we'd love to."

"If it's really no trouble . . . "

"Oh, no," Aldo assures her, "no trouble at all."

"Really? Thank you."

The girl thanks them again with a final big smile and goes out with her friend.

Silence follows this little scene. Total silence, given that Tiziana has switched off the radio. The old-timers, who were previously targeting Massimo and barking in unison like a pack of long-sighted wolves, are now each looking in a different direction and vaguely recalling a group of strangers waiting for the number 31 bus.

Massimo, on the other hand, takes a tray and quickly starts filling it. He leans under the counter to get a chinotto, saying as he does so, "Tiziana, one regular espresso and one with a shot of Sassolino. And then remind me that I have to go to the optician's."

"All right. Do you have problems?"

"No, no. I'm just going to buy a pair of blue contact lenses.

Maybe next time I ask for something, I'll flash my big blue eyes and somebody might actually listen to me."

"Maybe you should also hire a nice pair of boobs," Ampelio says in a surly tone. "You're already starting to talk as much crap as a woman."

"What would you like, Pilade?" Massimo asks casually from under the counter. "An amaro?"

"The trouble is, Massimo," Ampelio continues imperturbably, "that even with contact lenses, fake boobs and whatever, you were always ugly and you'll always be ugly."

"I know," Massimo says, reemerging from under the counter. "It runs in the family. We've been ugly for generations. With a few peaks, like Aunt Enza."

Massimo and his grandfather look at each other, and both start to laugh.

When Enza Viviani née Barontini, Ampelio's sister and Massimo's mother's aunt, came into the world, Signora Ofelia Viviani née Medori (Massimo's great-grandmother and Ampelio's mother, known to the whole family as "Ofelia of Windsor" because of the amount of gold and jewelry she would put on for solemn occasions) received visits from all the relatives and acquaintances, including Romualdo Griffa, Aldo's father and an old friend of the family. Romualdo, having bent over the crib and offered the infant a finger as big as a baguette, stood up again and thundered in a stentorian voice, "Dammit, Ofelia, congratulations. He really is a handsome boy."

"Look, Romualdo, she's a girl."

"Really?" Romualdo bent again over the crib, incredulous. "Dammit, poor little thing."

Getting back to the present day, even the other customers laugh, which is surprising, given that they know the story because Ampelio must have told it fifty times. Tiziana, who doesn't know the story, smiles, because she has understood that the storm has passed. With the same smile, she goes to Rimediotti, who in spite of everything is still grumbling, while the chinotto drips relentlessly from his effervescent hair. Flattering him with the very same smile, she lowers his head slightly, and dries his tuft. The old man, who, due to the position of his head, suddenly finds himself faced directly with Tiziana's chest, thanks her and turns red.

In short, now the storm has given way to a sense of calm, the climate is one of fraternal camaraderie, and thanks to Massimo's memory Ampelio now feels inclined to rake over the past and to start telling the thousands of stories he has about the days when he and the other doughty pensioners were young, or even earlier. Since the only thing that could stop Ampelio when he has decided to tell a story that goes back to the times of his remote youth would be military intervention by NATO, and given that our elderly hero is a narrator of undisputed talent, even if with a somewhat limited repertoire, the remaining bystanders happily get ready to listen to him.

Del Tacca, with a glass entirely of amaro in front of him, listens to Ampelio without looking up and chuckles to himself. Rimediotti and Aldo listen standing up, nodding sagely whenever Ampelio introduces a character from the past, to show that they remember him and that he really was a fine man. Tiziana listens with great amusement to the tall stories of this ribald old man whose memory is scandalously immune from the effects of age and hardened arteries. Every now and again, she glares at Massimo, who is still pretending to be working as a barman, cutting, pouring, washing, and moving things about, in order not to give his grandfather satisfaction, even though, in reality, he too is listening.

After a while, Ampelio starts to talk about the time he and Aldo worked in Pisa and, as a joke, replaced the menus dis-

played outside the tourist restaurants near Piazza dei Miracoli
with other homemade menus, which featured unlikely dishes
such as carpaccio of camel's ass and hair soup. Massimo, who
has heard the story umpteen times, takes a tray and goes outside to take the glasses emptied by the two girls who conquered the table under the elm.

He finds them in a state of great agitation.

The girl with the big eyes and her friend are clicking franti-
cally and opening all the files on the desktop, in search of
something they can't find. The girl with the big eyes has
despair written all over her face and is about to have an attack
of hysteria, while her friend sits huddled with a touching
expression very similar to that of a lost puppy. Shyly she asks
the other girl, "Are you sure it isn't there anymore?"

"Well, I can't find it. Look . . . How the hell . . . How is it
possible . . . It was here! It was here! Oh, my God . . . "

"If you'll allow me," Massimo says, taking the laptop from
the girl's hands and quickly placing it on one of the tables near
the tamarisks. The two girls are looking at him with stunned
expressions.

"Don't worry, there's no signal there. I couldn't help seeing
the screen. Some of the files have been corrupted. Have you
opened a window in a browser?"

"Y . . . yes," replies the buxom friend, because the girl with
the big eyes is still looking at Massimo as if he was a talking
rabbit. "I opened a window because I wanted to show her a
place in Barcelona, and after a while . . . I don't know, after a
while . . . "

"After a while, the window changed color and then froze."

"That's exactly it. The window turned green and . . . "

"Hmm. It's a virus that's been going around these last two
or three days. It only works if the computer is online, that's
why you don't have to worry now. Did you have any important
documents?"

The girl with the big eyes nods, still in a semi-catatonic state. "My presentation."

"What do you mean?"

"The presentation of my seminar. The papers that I was supposed to be doing the seminar with."

"That you're supposed to be doing a seminar with," Massimo repeats, a tad pedantically.

"That I was supposed to be doing the seminar with," the girl retorts, losing her temper. "That I was supposed to be doing the seminar with the day after tomorrow! And now what the hell—"

"Sorry if I'm asking pointless questions, but are you sure you haven't saved the seminar anywhere else?"

"No, why should I?"

"For many good reasons. What's just happened, for example."

The girl glares at him. "I've always worked on that computer. How am I supposed to know that you connect to the Internet and then there are sons of bitches who play tricks on you like that?"

Massimo might object that viruses like this have been doing the rounds for several years, and that ignoring their existence, if you own a computer, is the attitude of a Neanderthal. But, as someone having lived, Massimo knows perfectly well that arguing logically about a thoughtless act committed by a hysterical woman with that very same woman won't get you anywhere. So he chooses to be decisive.

"I'm quite familiar with the operating system you use. I think I might be able to recover a recent version of the file. When did you create it?"

"Let's see . . . a week ago, more or less."

"When was the last time you opened it?"

"It was open when this mess happened. Half an hour ago, I'd say. But look . . . "

Too late. Massimo has sat down in front of the laptop, and

now his fingers are dancing over the keyboard like little pink hammers in a strange, apparently senseless rhythm. The girl tries to say something, but Massimo silences her with a gesture of the hand while with the other he continues to beat out commands on the keyboard. Then he looks at Tiziana, who came out a few minutes ago and is now following the scene as a neutral observer.

"But . . . my computer . . . "

"Don't worry. Massimo's a genius with these gadgets."

"Yes, but—"

"In addition to anything else, he's a graduate. In mathematics. And one thing I can say is that I've known Massimo for a few years now, and although he has many faults, he never talks out of turn. If he's told you he can do it, he can."

"Yes, but—"

"Tiziana," Massimo says as his fingers continue to hammer the keys, "one of my many faults is that I find it hard to do things while people are standing over me. Can you all go inside, please?"

"But . . . " says the girl with the big eyes, then looks at Massimo and sees that he has recovered the file with her presentation. She is about to smile but Massimo stops her.

"I haven't finished yet. I need time. Please go inside."

Obediently, the girls follow Tiziana.

Half an hour later, the girl with the big eyes has calmed down. Her friend has stopped looking like an anxious puppy and is now wearing an expression of calm cheerfulness that suits her much better. In the meantime, the old-timers have come outside again, and, pretending that nothing has happened, have sat back down under the elm to play cards. The girls have stayed inside and are chatting about this and that with Tiziana when Massimo comes back into the bar with a satisfied smile. He hands the laptop to the girl.

"I think I've recovered everything. Please check."

The girl takes the computer, puts it on the counter, and runs the presentation from beginning to end. Strange square-shaped molecules appear on the screen, complex graphs, absorption spectrums of ultraviolet rays. All with a notable attention to design.

"I can't believe it! It's all there!"

"Are you sure? Have you checked everything?"

"Yes, yes. I'm sure. You've saved my life."

"Well, not your life exactly. But I have made your immediate future a little easier."

"Really, I . . . I don't know how to thank you."

Her friend speaks up. "I know a way."

For a moment, Massimo imagines the girl with the big eyes and her friend dressed only in whipped cream calling him from the bed in his apartment. But from the tone in which the girl has spoken, it's clear that she and Massimo haven't been thinking of the same thing. The friend looks at the bar and continues: "This place is really cute. Especially outside. We could have a party here after the dinner on Thursday. We'd have to make it clear, of course," she adds with a wink, "that whoever wants to come can come, but in a place like this and after dinner, well, obviously it should be just the young people. So, we come here, we socialize the way our director wants us to, and we get rid of all the senile old idiots. I don't know about you, but after a while I really can't stand all those old guys sitting at the table talking out of turn."

That makes two of us, Massimo thinks, looking outside toward his involuntary collection of living antiques.

"It's an idea . . . " says the girl with the big eyes.

"Look, let's do this," the other girl says with a determined air. "We'll tell the chief tonight, at the reception, and then tomorrow," she looks at Massimo, "we'll come straight back here and let you know."

"All right," Massimo replies. "If you decide before then, you can even let me know tonight. I'm going to be there with you."

"How do you mean?"

"You just said there's a reception tonight, and your friend was saying that she has to give a presentation the day after tomorrow. That means you're talking about a conference. As far as I know, the only conference in the vicinity is"—he takes a brochure from behind the counter—"the Twelfth International Workshop on Macromolecular and Biomacromolecular Chemistry—my God what a waste of capital letters—taking place at the Hotel Santa Bona in Pineta from May 21 to 26."

"Yes, that's right. But how did you come to have this brochure?"

"Because even conference delegates have to eat, and in such cases they turn to a catering service. And in this particular case, the catering service is being provided by me."

"You and Aldo," Tiziana cuts in.

"Yes, all right. Me and Aldo. Aldo's the gentleman outside with the white hair who's insulting the gentleman in the beret. We're in charge of the catering. That's why, unless anything untoward happens, I should also be at the conference tonight."

Two

D ays on which terrible things happen always begin like any other. Until something happens, they're just average days.

The first day of the Twelfth International Workshop, etc., etc., is no exception. Like any ordinary conference, at which no one is killed, it begins with a speaker of particular distinction who gives a lecture summing up his life's work. After this comes the first installment of seminars, which lasts from nine until eleven, followed by the first coffee break. Everything starts again at 11:30, and continues until lunchtime, when people usually have between one and two hours at their disposal. Finally, the conference resumes in the afternoon, continuing from 3:00 until 4:30, when there is a second coffee break, followed by the final installment of lectures, at the end of which, unfortunately, nothing has been planned.

Coffee breaks are essential for restoring the spirits of the conference delegates, exhausted by two hours of hard listening sitting on theater-style seats in a half-lit room. Usually in these circumstances, most of the academics lose every semblance of restraint: they hurl themselves at the trays, fill their plastic plates with precarious pyramids of breadsticks and sandwiches, and, gobbling down what they have conquered, listen to whichever colleague happens to have ended up next to them talking with their mouths full, while they chew enthusiastically.

In all this, Massimo and Aldo, impeccable in their uniforms—of waiter and maître d' respectively—are extras, acting at different speeds and in different styles: Massimo pours and Aldo decants, Massimo nods and Aldo approves, Aldo offers and Massimo serves. At first, obviously, they don't exchange a single word: they have to cope with the mad scramble of scientists. Subsequently, when most of the food has been plundered, the situation calms down and it becomes possible to exchange a few words.

"I didn't think there'd be so many people."

"There aren't so many really. Maybe about two hundred. I've seen conferences with more than a thousand people."

"A thousand people? I was thinking of those photographs of old conferences, the ones you see in the newspapers when there are anniversaries, obviously. The Solvay Conference, or something like that. Twenty, thirty people at most."

Aldo smiles and serves coffee to two Japanese who thank him and return his smile, then continues:

"Apart from anything else, not that I know about these things, but what's the point of a conference with a thousand delegates? How are you going to discuss anything?"

"This isn't the Congress of Vienna, Aldo. Anyway, to judge by the few I've been to, you don't really get serious discussions at conferences."

"You're right. There aren't many discussions at conferences. Could I have a coffee?"

The person who has spoken is a short man in a yellow T-shirt and a pair of surfing shorts. Although he spoke in Italian, his accent and appearance classify him as Nordic. Sure enough, the badge hanging from the bottom of his T-shirt identifies him as A. C. J. Snijders, Rijksuniversiteit Groningen, Netherlands. Massimo, who takes an immediate liking to him, pours what he has requested into a plastic cup and as he does so says, "If you can call this coffee . . . "

"Thanks. Look, as long as it has caffeine in it, it's fine by me. I need to wake up."

"Boring in there?"

"A little. The thing is, it's not my field. I'm a theoretician, and this morning it's the experimental scientists who are talking. The first speaker today, the one who opened the conference, was a theoretician. A really good one."

He takes a sip of his coffee, and makes a face that seems to mean: "It's not so bad."

"Kiminobu Asahara. A Japanese," he says as if this explains everything.

"Who's that?" Aldo butts in, just to have something to say.

"The old man over there, in that group. The tall one."

The little group indicated by Snijders is composed exclusively of Japanese men old enough to have bombed Pearl Harbor, so it's lucky that in pointing him out Snijders has specified that Asahara is tall. Sure enough, one of the elderly Orientals is a whole head taller than the group average. This particular individual has a glass in his hand and seems to be in a state of catalepsy: as he is being spoken to, his eyes close and his trunk leans forward slightly. The movement makes the liquid in the glass spill over a little, and (perhaps) because of the sudden cold he wakes up for some twenty seconds, then begins again to sink slowly into oblivion.

"What's he doing, sleeping?" Aldo asks.

"Pretty much. He falls asleep very easily. Even when he's speaking. And when he speaks his voice becomes ever more confused. During his lecture he must have lost consciousness a hundred times. It was torture. Ten seconds of silence and then one word. For some reason, they still get him to speak, an old man like that, I really don't know."

"Well, he must be an important person, probably highly respected," Aldo says, a touch acrimoniously, because he doesn't think it's such a terrible thing to be old.

"Oh, yes, he's important. He's done many good things as far as science goes. But it isn't right to get him to speak. People fall asleep. He should just be a presence, and that's all."

Snijders finishes his coffee in two gulps, then looks disconsolately at the gathered scientists. "Well, I think I've heard enough for this morning. Can you tell me if there are any free beaches around here?"

"Not around here, no," Aldo says. "There are the bathing establishments on the beach. You can hire an umbrella or a hut and you have access to the sea." As he speaks, he pours some fruit juice for a thin young woman who looks as if she has just come back from her cat's funeral and who according to her badge is Maria de Jesus Siqueira, Universidade de Coimbra, Portugal.

"And how much does it cost to hire an umbrella?" Snijders asks, in a tone that makes it clear that the cost of the hire might be crucial in establishing whether he likes this coast or not.

"I don't know, it depends. Between five and ten euros a day. Not so much," Aldo replies curtly, looking Snijders up and down as if asking himself if a man like this has ever seen ten euros together in one place in his life.

"Hmmm. That's quite expensive. Well, I could go back to the lecture . . . " Although he is still smiling, he doesn't seem very happy. The Portuguese woman, who is still standing there with her full glass in her hand, presumably not understanding anything, attempts a slight smile, which she then hides by drowning it in her fruit juice.

"If you're interested," Massimo says, "the hotel has a swimming pool. It's there behind the oleander hedges. It's reserved for guests of the hotel."

I'm a guest of the hotel, says the light that comes on in Snijders' eyes.

Sitting in the darkness of the conference hall, Koichi Kawaguchi was suffering terribly.

Firstly, he was suffering because of the lectures. All the lectures programmed for the day were being given by experimental chemists, and he was neither a chemist nor an experimenter. Koichi Kawaguchi was a computer expert, who, together with other researchers in his department, had developed a code for calculating the mechanical properties of polymer-based composites. Since this code could in principle be used—and would be coveted—by all those doing research in the field of macromolecules, his department had sent a representative to present the code and do a little publicity at every conference touching on the subject of polymers, even if only remotely. Including the present conference, whose central theme was the synthesis and characterization of functionalized and biofunctionalized polymers. In other words, things in which Koichi did not have the slightest interest, studied by people who were presumably not interested in his code.

Therefore, what lay in store for Koichi was a conference in which he would spend the oral sessions (skipping the lectures was out of the question) listening to reports of which he understood nothing and which in any case did not interest him in the slightest.

But this, Koichi could stand.

Something else that lay in store for Koichi was the prospect of spending the whole round of poster sessions standing by his poster in jacket and tie, as Japanese custom demanded of all those presenting their work either with a poster or in an oral session. A poster in front of which, presumably, nobody would stop, obliging Koichi to spend a few humiliating hours simply standing still and waiting.

But even this, Koichi could stand.

All this would be taking place in the conference hall of the Hotel Santa Bona, whose stiff plastic chairs combined admirably with the irregular functioning of the air-conditioning to annoy the conference delegates, who, for the ten minutes during which the air-conditioning was on vacation sweated like marathon runners, and for the following ten (in which the system, probably feeling guilty, tried to recover credibility by vigorously blowing cold air into the room) risked pathologies ranging from pleuritis to acute lumbago.

But even this, Koichi could have stood.

What he really couldn't stand was the fact that the conference hall of the hotel had a glass wall. And through the glass wall you could see an oleander hedge. A few minutes earlier, Koichi had seen that strange Dutch professor disappear behind the oleander hedge, in swimming trunks and inflatable ring cushion, with a book in his hand. And now, through the gaps in the hedge, the placid figure of A. C. J. Snijders was visible from time to time, sitting in the ring, supporting the book with one hand and trailing the other in the water, clearly at peace with the world and with himself.

"Do you think they're going to finish everything?"

"I have no idea. If they do, they have my admiration. And I'll put flowers on their graves."

"All right, don't exaggerate now."

"I'm not exaggerating. Look at how much stuff there is. If these old guys really finish everything, one or two of them are bound to die on us."

It was 4:30 in the afternoon, and while the first part of the afternoon session of the conference was taking place, under the mysterious title *Protein Binding, Folding and Recognition*, Massimo and Aldo were finishing laying the tables by the swimming pool with the trays and carafes intended for the scientists' snack.

The culinary part of the afternoon had been personally taken care of by Tavolone, the chef from Aldo's restaurant and a firm believer in the equation: quantity equals quality.

Faced with the task of organizing a mid-afternoon aperitif/snack/tasting session, Tavolone had had the idea of exploiting his recent vacation in Spain and cramming the hundred square feet of tables at his disposal with a magnificent array of tapas of all kinds. From behind his table, Massimo salivated as he gazed at the ranks of multicolored delicacies: potato tortillas, creamed cod canapés, little sausages dressed in layers of artichoke, broccoli tops wrapped in bacon and sprinkled with granules of crisp baby onion, small tomatoes stuffed with goat's cheese and parsley, and so on. They cheered you up just to look at them. And made you hungry, of course. Not that it took much to make Massimo hungry. After all, he was Ampelio's grandson, and blood was thicker than water.

But the food had been arranged too well. Too tidily, in compact, symmetrical piles. It wasn't possible to take a single thing out before the crowd arrived without leaving an obvious hole. That was why Massimo was trying to evaluate how likely it was that the delegates would leave any survivors that could then be taken prisoner and executed after everything had been put away, maybe enjoying the coolness of seven o'clock in the evening sitting on a deck chair next to the swimming pool without a thought in the world. Tiziana would be in the bar until eight. On the other hand, the scientists had already given proof of their talent that morning, when they had raided the tables during the coffee break and left nothing behind but crumpled napkins and a little fruit juice at the bottoms of the glasses.

To distract himself from the thought of food, once everything was ready for the beginning of the break, Massimo had sat down with the earphones of his iPod in his ears, and was enjoying a nice mix of hits from the 80s to the present day.

While Massimo was listening, slumped in his plastic chair, Aldo had taken from his pocket a pack of poker cards, still in its glossy cardboard wrapper. He opened it, took out the pack, and spread it in a perfect textbook fan, with every card showing on the corner the suit and the value before being covered by the preceding one. He closed the pack, cut it, and shuffled it American-style. Then he took a card from the pack and showed it to Massimo with the air of someone who is about to do something amazing, but he must have changed his mind because he almost immediately replaced it and put the pack down behind the table.

"Here they come. Get up, take those things out of your ears and give me a hand."

"No trick for Massimo?"

"No. I'll do it later, if you're good. Right now, the barbarians are arriving."

Sure enough, the glass doors that gave onto the terrace had opened, and from the conference hall the scholars were scattering into the open air, following different trajectories. Some lingered to talk with colleagues about proteins, while others headed resolutely toward the table laden with carbohydrates. Still others, having taken laptops from their bags, looked for a quiet corner in which there was a good enough wi-fi signal to check their mail and see if, in their absence, the world was still turning. Some did it earlier, some later, but all of them somehow found a way to come to the tables and fill their plates as they were entitled to do, while Massimo and Aldo poured, served, and waited.

"It seems you're not the only one with nimble hands in this place," Massimo said after a while.

"What?"

"Those German guys just in front of us, the one with the white shirt and the one with the crew cut. I heard them say a computer was stolen this morning during the break."

"Ah. Honest people, these scientists."

"Not necessarily. It could have been anyone. Maybe someone from the hotel."

"You're right," Aldo replied. "It could have been anyone. Even your friend."

"My friend?"

"Yes, the one who hates old people," Aldo said with a wink.

Massimo followed the direction of his gaze. Not far from them, A. C. J. Snijders was conversing calmly with a group of young people and sipping a glass of mineral water.

"It seems to me the feeling is mutual," Massimo said, watching with growing frustration as the canapés on the trays gradually but inexorably disappeared. The creamed cod in particular, which aroused all Massimo's gluttony and had been making his mouth water ever since they had laid the tables, seemed one of the most frequently requested, and there was little hope now that a few small pieces might escape the attention of the delegates.

"Come on, now," Aldo said after handing a napkin to a middle-aged Frenchwoman who had spilled her coffee all over her clothes. "Apart from anything else, you need a little self-respect. Do you really think it's right for a university professor to go around the world like that? He looks as if he's just been released from prison."

"The way someone dresses is irrelevant," Massimo said, shooting another glance at Snijders, who did actually give the impression not so much that he had dressed of his own free will as that he had been assaulted by his own clothes. "It's the brain that counts. And besides, as long as you don't harm anybody, I don't mind if you go around with your ass covered in blue paint."

"Don't say that too loudly. Somebody might take you seriously. Actually, I don't see that tall Japanese fellow."

"Right. I don't think he was feeling well."

"What?"

"Some of the guys who were standing here before mentioned the fact that someone called Asahara hurt himself just after lunch. He slipped on a rug in his room and hit his head on a chest of drawers. I'm sure the old Japanese man the guy today was talking about was called Asahara. Anyway, slipping on a rug seems to me the kind of thing he'd do. That's why I think it must be him. Nothing serious, apparently. He just hurt himself and they took him to Emergency to give him some stitches."

"Poor man. I'm sorry," Aldo said in a tone of voice that made it clear he didn't give a damn about the Asaharas of this world.

"Me too," Massimo replied sincerely, watching resignedly as a female hand reached out across the tray and grabbed the last creamed cod canapé. He followed the hand on its journey toward its owner's mouth, and was repaid by the fact that the mouth in question belonged to a really pretty girl. Not just pretty, beautiful. Blonde hair, narrow blue eyes, arched eyebrows. Elegant, but not off-puttingly so. She probably also had a beautiful smile: Massimo could only hypothesize this given that the blonde had just swallowed the canapé and was chewing energetically, but a girl like that must have a beautiful smile. She was the kind of girl you wanted to tell the story of your life to.

Little by little, without any signal or announcement, the delegates started to move toward the conference hall. As they went back in, Massimo followed the blonde with his eyes for a few seconds, trying to see from her badge what her name was and where she came from. But to no avail. Paradoxically, he did not linger over the rest of her person. Someone with a face as beautiful as that could be as flat as a plank as far as Massimo was concerned.

He watched the delegates enter the conference hall, and through the glass door saw one of the organizers take the microphone, grim-faced, and say a few words. As he spoke, the delegates started looking at one another incredulously.

"Massimo, wake up. We have to clear all this."

Massimo turned. Aldo had rolled up his shirtsleeves above his elbows (oh, yes, you talk about style and then you roll up your sleeves) and had started to gather the remains of napkins, cocktail sticks, and so on from the table.

"I'm sorry. I was distracted for a moment. I don't know what's going on in there."

"Where?"

"In the conference hall. Something must have happened."

Sure enough, many people had stood up and started talking among themselves, while the speaker had left the microphone on the table and joined one of the groups. Automatically, Aldo buttoned up the cuffs of his shirt and headed toward the hall. Just imagine if he minded his own business for once, Massimo thought, and started to tidy up, beginning by piling up the trays.

After about a minute, Aldo came back. He again unbuttoned his cuffs and looked at Massimo like someone who has something to say. Massimo looked at him and put the trays to one side.

"What happened?" he asked without further ado, given that it was obvious that something had happened.

"If I understood correctly . . . " Aldo began, and stopped.

"If you understood correctly?"

"That Japanese man, Asahara. Seems like he's dead."

THREE

T he alarm clock. Is that the alarm clock? Shit. Come on, let's get up. But why is it so dark outside? Is it the weather? Oh, my God, look how it's raining. It's pouring down. Great! All right, a quick coffee and then I'm off.

Standing by the window in the living room of his apartment, with a cup of coffee in his hand, Massimo watched the rain descending, like big ropes of water beating down on the street. He had woken up in a good mood, amid the last traces of a dream in which he was flying, and whenever Massimo dreamed about flying he always woke up well disposed toward the world. The sight of the rain had not dispelled his good mood. On the contrary, that heavy but thunderless downpour galvanized him and made him feel alive. That had happened even when he was little, and he had to go to school in the deluge: it was always a special morning, and as he walked to school, savoring in advance the comfort of the warm, dry classroom, he would feel like some kind of heroic traveler lost in the storm.

Having arrived at the bar, he took off his oilskin and his rain pants, put them in a plastic bag, and left it in the storeroom, then began the ritual round of Things to Do. Every morning, in fact, when he got to the bar, Massimo always did exactly the same things in exactly the same order. *Est modus in rebus.*

First, he switched on the coffee machine, which started up with its usual gurgling hiss, breaking the absolute silence that reigned in the bar. Then he switched on the oven, the ice cream cabinet, and the dishwasher, after which he arranged the tables and chairs inside the bar, while the outside furniture, as always when it rained, was put in the storeroom as a punishment. Only then did he switch on the lights: that way he was always confronted with a bar that already looked bright and in working order. Last but not least, having taken the *Gazzetta dello Sport* from the letter box—the news vendor brought it at 6:30 every morning—he sat down at a table with a glass of iced tea and immersed himself in the paper. This was by far the best moment of his day. On his own, without a thought in his head, and at peace with himself and with the world.

Beata solitudo, sola beatitudo.

At that moment, the telephone rang.

Massimo looked toward the back of the bar, where the evil device was located.

The telephone's only response was to continue ringing with cruel indifference, its sound similar to the noise made when you let down a bucket into a well, and the chain grates against the pulley, and the bucket goes lower and lower, just like Massimo's mood.

You couldn't ignore the telephone. Massimo had never been able to. Massimo could ignore people, deadlines, politeness, bureaucracy (when it didn't concern the bar), and many other things he considered unworthy of his attention, but when the telephone rang, he had to answer it. Reluctantly, walking deliberately slowly, because maybe that way whoever the son of a bitch was would be convinced that there was nobody there and put the receiver down, which would mean it wasn't anything important anyway. Or maybe it was Tiziana phoning to say she was sick and couldn't come in to work, and that would bring Massimo's mood down even more.

He got to the phone and lifted the receiver. "Good morning, Bar Lume."

A voice with a Venetian accent said, "Is that the Bar Lume?"

"Yes, it's still the Bar Lume. I haven't moved the phone in the last two seconds."

"Pineta Police Station here. Are you Signor Massimo Viviani?"

The police station. What now?

"Yes, this is he."

"Inspector Fusco would like to speak with you. Could you hold on a moment, please?"

"All right."

Fusco. Oh, God. An unsound mind in an unhealthy body.

Inspector Vinicio Fusco aroused both irritation and a kind of compassion in Massimo. The mixture of arrogance, pretentiousness, stupidity and stubbornness, all compacted together with dubious taste into a block no more than five feet tall, that was Vinicio Fusco was something he found at once sad and tiresome. And, as always happens with people we don't like, even characteristics that in themselves were of no intrinsic significance, such as his height, became unforgivable defects, as well as excellent pretexts for taking the mickey out of the individual in question.

"Good morning, Signor Viviani," came Fusco's voice.

"It was," Massimo replied, thinking of the *Gazzetta*.

"I need to speak to you as soon as possible. Can you come to the station?"

"Not right now. I'm alone in the bar. I have to wait for Tiziana to get here."

"Will she be much longer?"

"I don't think so. She should be here around seven."

"Excellent. As soon as Signorina Guazzelli arrives, I'd like you to come to the station."

"All right. Could you at least tell me—"

"I'll tell you everything at the station, don't worry," Fusco said in a tone in which Massimo thought he heard a touch of sarcasm. "Good morning."

Good morning my ass, Massimo thought, while the *Gazzetta* looked up at him with a disconsolate air. Now I have to get dressed again, plunge into the storm, and go to hear what that ballbreaker wants. What the hell, until Tiziana gets here, I can read the paper for a while.

Massimo sat down again comfortably, took a sip of tea, and opened the *Gazzetta* with renewed care. At that moment, the door opened and a strange creature came in, green in color, about six feet tall, pear-shaped, with two arms but no legs, and soaking wet.

"What a downpour!" the creature said. "Did you see it?"

Hearing the voice, Massimo realized that his childhood dream of meeting a Barbapapa for real was not about to come true, and that the organism that had just come in through the door was in fact Tiziana, wrapped in a huge raincoat that went all the way down to her feet and with a hood that hid her face. Disappointed, partly because now that Tiziana had arrived he would have to get up, Massimo closed the newspaper.

"I saw it and heard it," he said, standing up, while Tiziana divested herself of her deep-sea diver's costume and stuffed it into a rucksack.

"Oh, my God! It's going to take me a moment to change. With this shroud on me, I've been sweating like a pig. Then I'll see to the croissants and things. You stay there and finish your paper, if you want."

"If only!" Massimo said. "I have to go to the police station."

"The police station?"

"Fusco phoned me about five minutes ago."

"What does he want?"

"To break my balls, I guess. Apart from that I have no idea. He wouldn't tell me a thing."

"Nice man."

"As always."

Massimo put his rainproof gear back on and looked outside. The police station was a few hundred yards away, if you took the shortcut through the pine grove, or just under two miles, if you went by car. All right, come on. Let's walk through the pine grove in the storm. Get going, Indiana Jones.

Massimo's reluctance to take his car was mainly due to the new system with which the traffic department of the municipality of Pineta had sought, it wasn't quite clear how, to improve the traffic of the town or, to use the words of the head of the department, the urban conglomeration.

Heedless of the presence of brains in their own craniums, the members of the department had planned and realized a series of insane changes, without any concern for the fact that a street network should be there to allow vehicles to travel, and not to serve the sick fantasies of self-styled Le Corbusiers with all the practical sense of guinea fowls. All this without taking into account the fact that the working of Pineta's street network was the least of the few problems affecting the town. Pardon, the urban conglomeration. For example, one of the fundamental improvements that had been made to the streets of Pineta had been the so-called "Provision of seven miles of bicycle lanes in the area adjacent and parallel to Viale dei Cardi and Via del Lungomare, and modification of the signage in accordance with the current European standards on urban routes intended for velocipedes."

What this meant in practice was that the sidewalks of the streets running alongside the sea and those leading into them had been adorned with yellow lines that ran parallel to the bottoms of the buildings, as well as a few signs showing a man on a bicycle and shamelessly renamed "bicycle lanes."

With this stroke of genius, the municipality had managed to expropriate the money that the European Community, systematically underestimating the imagination and inventiveness of the Italian mind, had earmarked for the provision of bicycle lanes, giving so much per mile of lane installed. The fact that cobbled sidewalks were not ideal for bicycles, as well as the fact that there were already natural bicycle lanes, amply exploited by the townspeople, in the form of the paths that wound through the pine grove, had not affected the municipality's plans in the slightest. In any case, the locals had continued happily using the paths and the unfortunate Pineta-Roubaix cycling track was used only by tourists, giving rise to the occasional accident.

For this and other reasons, driving a car in the middle of Pineta had become a kind of obstacle course, and Massimo tried to avoid it whenever he could. And so, again wrapping himself in his oilskin sarcophagus, he set out for the police station.

As he walked through the storm, the rain so strong that he could distinctly feel the liquid smack of each drop on his skin through the raincoat, Massimo was thinking about what reason Fusco could possibly have to summon him. And as often happened when he was alone, he thought out loud and his thoughts started to drift.

"So. For Fusco to call me at this hour it must be something important . . . And something criminal . . . Not the bar. It can't have anything to do with the bar. There haven't been any shady characters using the bar for a long time . . . apart from Councilor Curioni, of course . . . he'd sell his own father to get votes, if he could find him . . . I wonder how some people manage to sleep at night . . . and he's so vulgar . . . how can somebody so ignorant become a politician? . . . No, better not to think about it . . . it'll only make my blood boil . . . I graduated college and I'm working as a barman, whereas a man like that who wouldn't know a subjunctive if it hit him in the eye is a councilor . . . Let's get back to us. I haven't murdered anybody.

My grandfather must have wished a few thousand people dead, but that's no crime . . . I can't see Tiziana killing anyone . . . What else have I done lately? Almost nothing . . . I'm still at the conference . . . Oh, my God, the conference . . . Something happened at the conference . . . Something happened, yes, shit, a man died . . . But from natural causes . . . I don't see why Fusco should be involved . . . Inspector Fusco . . . Strange, I don't even need to call him Inspector Fusco to distinguish him from any other Fusco . . . there's only one Fusco . . . thank goodness for that . . . Oh, look, we're here . . ."

As soon as Massimo walked into the police station, dripping water like a giant umbrella, a young, skinny, bespectacled officer, a kind of seminarian in uniform, emerged from the porter's lodge and came up to him.

"Massimo Viviani?" the officer asked, in the same Venetian-accented voice Massimo had earlier heard on the phone.

"All present and correct."

"Good morning. I'm Officer Galan. Inspector Fusco has asked me to take you straight to him. This way, please."

Still dripping, Massimo entered the office of Inspector Fusco—or Dr. Fusco, as the inspector, having a degree, liked to think of himself—and stopped just inside the doorway. Standing there by the window, looking out in silence, was the man himself.

Since Fusco was not saying a word, Massimo started taking off his raincoat. As he was trying to separate his shoes from the hems of his pants, Fusco turned and looked at him for a moment, then turned back to the window and said, "Do you know the law, Signor Viviani?"

"More or less."

I know the basics, Massimo thought as he finished extracting his own foot from the cloth trap. Whereas you don't even know the basics of politeness. Good morning, please take a seat, I'm sorry to have made you come here at this ungodly hour, especially in a hurricane. That's the least to expect. Go figure.

Fusco moved away from the window and starting walking up and down the room. "The law," he resumed, "says that when a person dies, a doctor must ascertain the cause of death. And if the cause of death is clear, he issues a certificate, and that's the end of it. If on the other hand it isn't clear, or can't immediately be attributed to natural causes, the doctor doesn't sign the death certificate and calls in the legal authorities."

All well and good, Massimo thought. And why should I give a damn?

"That's why, just to take a random example, if an elderly Japanese professor, just to give him a nationality, dies after hitting his head on the edge of a piece of furniture, the doctor can either sign the certificate or not sign it. And if he doesn't sign it, he calls in the legal authorities. In other words, me."

Oh, shit.

"Now, this is how things stand. Professor"—Fusco looked at a sheet of paper—"Ki-mi-no-bu A-sa-ha-ra, seventy-four years old, was pronounced dead yesterday afternoon at Santa Chiara Hospital in Pisa from respiratory arrest following a severe cranial trauma."

"I'm sorry," Massimo said. "I didn't quite catch that. Respiratory arrest following a cranial trauma?"

Fusco raised his cowlike eyes and looked at him. "Precisely. In practical terms, the poor man slipped on a rug and hit his head. Following the blow, he seemed confused, and so his colleagues thought it wise to take him to the hospital. But he never got to the hospital, or rather, he was dead by the time he got there. The doctor who saw him established that he was dead. Initial examination suggested that death was due to respiratory arrest."

"I don't understand."

"Neither do I. And neither did the doctor. That's why, along with Dr. Cattoni, our pathologist, he ordered a post-mortem."

Fusco went to the desk and rested his buttocks on the edge, directly facing Massimo.

"I don't yet have the postmortem report, so there's nothing official. But in essence, the two doctors agreed that a sudden respiratory arrest in a man in good health is somewhat unlikely, and so they looked for a cause. By chance, they found a card with medical instructions in the professor's billfold. You know, one of those cards epileptics carry with them, or people who have some disease or allergy that means they absolutely have to avoid certain medicines, and which describe what to do if they have an attack. To cut a long story short, Professor Asahara suffered from quite a rare neurological disease called . . . "—Fusco consulted the sheet of paper—" . . . called myasthenia gravis. And here comes the good part."

"Which is?" Massimo asked, since Fusco seemed to need encouraging.

"Which is that, as if things weren't already complicated enough, the doctors still aren't happy. The disease is one thing, they say, but the dead man's general condition wasn't compatible with a death of that kind. He didn't have one foot in the grave. He walked around, gave lectures, didn't have any obvious symptoms of the disease. In other words, as far as the doctors are concerned, if he'd only had that disease, the professor, who was otherwise in excellent health, would have lasted quite a while longer."

Remarkable, Massimo thought. A man who looked about a hundred and six and could barely keep awake was, according to the doctors, in the peak of condition. What constitutions the Japanese have. Obviously sushi, green tea, and puffer fish keep you fit even if you lead a crap life. Getting up in the morning, the subway, the work, the bowing . . . Fortunately, while one hemisphere of Massimo's brain was coming up with this stream of nonsense, the other woke up suddenly and suggested a possible reason for Fusco to have summoned him.

"To cut a long story short," Fusco went on, "the blood tests show that the dead man had taken a massive dose of lorazepam, which is a kind of tranquilizer."

I know it. They sell it as Tavor.

"In other words, a drug that no conscientious doctor would ever have prescribed for a patient with the illness I mentioned earlier. Apart from anything else, from a few discreet questions asked of some of his colleagues, it seems there's nothing to indicate that the professor ever suffered from anxiety attacks, depression, or any other behavioral disorders."

"I get it," Massimo said. Oh, yes, he thought, give me a prize. At least my brain's still working.

"And there you are." Fusco got up from the edge of the desk and went and sat down behind it. "According to the doctors, in a man suffering from myasthenia gravis, a drug like lorazepam can cause motor difficulties and mental confusion. That explains both why the poor man slipped and also why after slipping, and probably even earlier, he seemed a little dazed. But above all, if the patient falls asleep or loses consciousness, the drug can cause respiratory arrest."

Which explains the death, Massimo thought without saying it.

Fusco was silent for a moment, looked at the palms of his hands, sighed, then resumed, "Now, I realize there isn't anything official yet, but as you know, in some things timing is of the essence. I can't wait for the postmortem report to . . . "—and here Fusco broke off, looked away from Massimo, and made a sign with his hand that seemed to mean, "Just look what a mess I've gotten myself into."

Massimo met him halfway. "To ask me if, from behind the

tables, I saw someone put something in a glass and take it to Professor Asahara during the coffee break?"

"That's exactly it. As I'm sure you realize, I don't have any reason to ask you this officially. But the more time I let pass, the likelier it is that you'll forget what you saw during the break. If you saw anything, of course. That's why I asked you to come here."

You got it, Fusco, Massimo thought. This time you took aim and hit the target. Congratulations. But that was all. Massimo was in no position to help him.

"I understand. I didn't see anything. But that doesn't mean that nothing happened. On the contrary. When the break starts, people crowd around the refreshment tables. For a few minutes, there are about twenty people at each table, and they're constantly changing. I can't rule out the possibility that it happened there."

I can't rule out the possibility that it happened there or I can't rule out the possibility that it didn't happen there? Maybe both.

"I see," Fusco said. "Actually, I didn't expect a different answer. Well, let's say I was hoping for one, but hope doesn't get you very far . . . Anyway, I have neither the intention nor the possibility of questioning you now. If there's an investigation, of course, I'll have to question you officially. That's why I must ask you to try to remember even the smallest detail that may have struck you."

"I'll try. But . . . "

"In any case, I must also ask you not to say a word to anybody about what I've told you. For the moment, I repeat, there's nothing official. There might well be another explanation for the whole thing. Although I doubt it. So, not a word about this, please."

"Of course. Don't worry."

Fusco nodded, then pressed a button on his intercom. After

a few seconds, the door of the office opened and the unmistakable seminarian's voice said devoutly, "Yes, sir?"

"Good morning, Galan. Please see Signor Viviani out and bring the other one in here."

As the ineffable Galan was carrying him in procession to the exit, Massimo saw Aldo sitting in the waiting room, calmly reading a glossy magazine. Seeing Massimo, Aldo closed the magazine and stood up. He didn't seem surprised.

"Good morning, Aldo. I didn't know you enjoyed reading that crap."

"What, this?" Aldo said, looking at the first page of the magazine, which promised the inside scoop on the love lives of TV personalities and heirs to the throne throughout the world. "I found it here. I usually read the *Corriere della Sera*. I got it this morning and put it in my pocket. Then I walked here in the rain. Right now I have a watery seven percent solution of newspaper in my pocket. Did Fusco ask you about the dead man at the conference?"

"I'm sorry," the seminarian cut in as Massimo was about to open his mouth, "I don't think it's right for two people who've been summoned here to confer among themselves. Please follow me, Signor Griffa."

"I'm coming, I'm coming. 'Bye, Massimo. See you at the bar."

FOUR

Tragedy at the Conference, Professor Hits His Head and Dies. By Pericle Bartolini.' Poor guy, whenever anything terrible happens, they always send him. Even the priest turns tail and runs when he sees him. 'Pineta. It seemed like a simple accident, but what happened yesterday at the Hotel Santa Bona soon turned to tragedy. The first day of the Twelfth International Conference on Macrolecul, no, Macromolecul and Biomacro . . . ,' anyway, you know the one he means, 'was coming to an end when the audience of scientists was informed by one of the organizers of the sudden death of . . . '"—Ampelio paused—"' . . . Kiimiinoobu Asaahara, a Japanese scientist known throughout the world for his work in the field of biotechnology. After lunch, Professor Asahara had suffered what at first was considered merely a small accident.' Put like that, anyone'd think he shit in his pants. 'Having apparently slipped on a rug, he had hit his head on the edge of a piece of furniture, suffering contusions to the side of his skull. A simple accident indeed. But, as he was being taken to his room as a precautionary measure, the elderly professor suddenly lost consciousness. Having been informed by telephone, the doctors in Emergency,' the ones who were in the bar, 'could do nothing but advise those with the professor to wait for an ambulance. Unfortunately, they could not postpone the inevitable.'"

Inevitable. That's the word. Just like these old codgers' fascination with death. Why do they always start with the deaths and disasters when they read the paper? Maybe they're keeping score. Oh, look, they've just buried another one. Ampelio: six thousand one hundred and twelve, rest of the world: zero. It must be the age. Maybe every day they find it more and more unlikely that they're still alive. Talking of unlikely things, we're starting to wallow in them here. Two murders two summers running, in a town with a population of five thousand. We're going to end up like the town where the main character lives in *Murder, She Wrote*, a town of only three thousand people where every day one of them gets murdered, and then every now and again the main character is invited somewhere to spend the weekend and bang! Somebody's murdered there too. How come they never realize the old biddy brings bad luck? Why are they always inviting her?

While Massimo's brain was wandering incoherently, not needing to help his body, which was busy loading the dishwasher, Ampelio continued reading, as usual interspersing the contents of the article with his own comments:

"'By the time the ambulance finally arrived, the situation was beyond anyone's control. At the ER, it was found that the elderly professor was already dead, and the doctors could do nothing but verify the fact.' And then they all went back to the bar."

"How old was he?" Del Tacca asked, putting sugar in his coffee.

"Seventy-four," Ampelio replied, folding the newspaper.

"Young."

"Oh, yes," Massimo laughed as he finished putting the coffee spoons in the drum. "His nanny strangled him."

"What are you trying to say? That just because Pilade is seventy-five he's lived too long? I'm eighty-three, what are you planning to do, beat me to death?"

There are times when I'd really like to, Massimo thought as he tried to insert the drum filled with dishes into the jaws of the monster, each failed attempt causing a tremendous clatter of flatware.

"It was a joke. Just like yours. A man of seventy-four isn't young."

"It depends. You're thirty-seven and you seem older than any of us."

Why are they always picking on me? Massimo was about to reply, when he was interrupted by the noise of pouring rain, immediately followed by Aldo coming into the bar.

"Greetings, everyone," he said, taking off his raincoat. "What's up?"

"What's up is that you could at least be on time for once," Del Tacca said. "We've been waiting an hour for you."

"I'm sorry. I didn't know going to a bar was considered a job."

"Maybe you didn't," Ampelio sneered, "but Pilade used to work at the town hall."

"Anyway, I've a good reason for being late," Aldo said. "As a good citizen, I was asked to lend my services to the civil authorities. The same request was made to our worthy barman, who's glaring at me right now. Isn't Rimediotti here yet?"

News, the old-timers' faces were saying. Fresh news just in. When one of them asks in that tone of feigned indifference if so-and-so is here yet, it means he has something to report and needs the largest possible audience.

"Never mind. Massimo, will you make me a coffee?"

"No, but I will ask you a question," Massimo said, having started the dishwasher and now putting the croissants in the oven in the back room. "Weren't we supposed to keep quiet about this?"

Aldo looked at him for a moment, then leaned across the counter to take Massimo's pack of cigarettes.

"Massimo, when I was ten years old I realized that in order to live well I shouldn't listen to what my father and mother said. When I was thirty, if I was going to keep enjoying life, there was no way I was about to listen to what my wife said. When I turned sixty, I had to start ignoring the doctor too. So now I'm seventy-two, do you really think I should do what Fusco tells me? Can I cadge a cigarette, mine are a bit wet."

Fusco, Ampelio and Pilade silently repeated to each other, looking each other in the eyes, Crime news. Sounds promising.

"Rimediotti won't be coming today anyway," Pilade said, settling comfortably in his chair. "It's so damp, his back must be killing him."

Which meant, implicitly: We're all here. There's no need to wait for anybody else. Come on, out with it.

"Well, this morning I was asleep and the phone rings. I go to answer, and a very, very mild voice asks me if I can come to the police station. Outside it's already raining cats and dogs. Why? I ask. We'll tell you when you get here, he answers. Do I have to come right away or can I wait until the animals leave the ark, I ask. It's an urgent matter, so we'd be grateful if you could come right away, the mild little voice answers. Oh, Tiziana, please, since Massimo won't make me a coffee, would you make me one?"

"Right away," Tiziana says, heading straight for the machine, eager to get it done quickly so as not to miss anything.

"So I put on my coat and go to the police station. And there I'm greeted by this nice young policeman who says, 'If you don't mind waiting, right now the inspector is conferring with another person regarding the matter.' Fine, I sit down. After a while, the door of the inspector's office opens and who do you think comes out?"

"Massimo, who else?" Tiziana said, handing the coffee to Aldo, thus ruining the climax of his story.

"Massimo?" Pilade said in surpise. "So you were serious earlier, Tiziana?"

"When I told you he was at the police station? Of course I was serious!"

"How was I supposed to know? I thought you were joking."

"Anyway," Aldo went on, resuming the reins, "I see Massimo and I put two and two together. Why call both me and Massimo? Because we're both involved with the catering for the conference. So something must have happened at the conference."

"I don't believe it!" Ampelio cried. "The dead Japanese! Was he murdered?"

"Ampelio, the Japanese died because he tripped over a rug and hit his head," Pilade said, silencing him with his supposed authority. "How could somebody have murdered him? Did they disguise themselves as a rug and trip him up?"

"No," Aldo said gravely, while Pilade and Tiziana laughed. "From what Fusco says, it was a lot simpler than that. Somebody poisoned him."

"Come on, smart-ass!" Ampelio said, also laughing. "What's poison got to do with it? Are there poisons you can give to people that make them trip up? Pull the other one."

"No, idiot. Just listen to me or we'll be here all day. Apparently this guy, who by the way in my opinion was already half dead anyway, died from respiratory arrest. He hit his head, they took him to the hospital, and there he died of respiratory arrest."

"All right," Del Tacca said, stubbornly. "So?"

"Do you think that's normal, Pilade?" Aldo picked up the cigarette he had put on the table and lit it. "You hit your head and you choke to death? What are the odds?"

"I don't know what the odds are," Massimo is watching the croissants get nice and golden in the discreet yellow light of the oven. "But the odds in here are that you shouldn't be smoking."

"Oh, come on, Massimo, it's like Hurricane Katrina out-side. There's nobody about. Who do you think's going to come in and say something?"

"I don't think anyone's going to come in. But you know how it is. We're in a bar, and one thing you can't deny about a bar is that it's a public place. And in public places, you can't smoke."

"There's something we could do about that," Ampelio said. "We could make it a private club instead of a bar. Then it wouldn't be a public place anymore, and we could all smoke in peace."

"Don't even think about it. Apart from the fact that if I started a private club, I'd join the Foreign Legion before I'd make you a member. Anyway," Massimo turned back to Aldo, "right now, this is a bar. If they come in and catch you, we'll both be fined. I don't give a damn about you, but I don't see why I should be involved. Do you smoke in your restaurant?"

"It's already lit," Aldo said fatalistically, as if it had been the will of Manitou that had lit the cigarette. "If a cop comes in, I'll pay the fine for both of us. Just stop interrupting. Anyway, the doctor saw how the man had died and got suspicious. So he ordered a postmortem. To cut a long story short, the guy had a whole lot of Tavor in his system. That's what caused him to stop breathing."

"I see. So?"

"What do you mean, 'so'? He'd been given a pile of Tavor and it had poisoned him."

"Right." Pilade, now safe in the immunity established by Aldo, picked up the pack of unfiltered Stop and took one out. "And who says he was given it deliberately to poison him? My poor brother Remo took Tavor for ten years, and nothing ever happened to him. Apart from the fact that he became senile, poor man, but that was age, not the Tavor."

One basic technique, in the professional practice of bar talk, consists of objecting to a fact or an argument with an appropriate counterexample, all the better if it refers to events that happened to a close relative, preferably now dead. In some way that's not quite clear, close kinship, according to the oral tradition prevalent in the town, guarantees the authenticity of what you're saying, and at the same time the unavailability of the protagonist of the example due to death makes it hard to refute.

As it happens, Pilade's example, unlike those generally used in bar discussions, was quite relevant. He could even have been right, which would have meant there had been no murder. What a pity, Ampelio's face seemed to say, it was just starting to get interesting. Fortunately, Aldo knew his facts and came back to the attack.

"It's the doctor that says it. The poor man was sick, and couldn't take Tavor. For him it was like poison. From what Fusco told me, not even Dr. Mengele would have prescribed it. The doctor's in no doubt. He was poisoned. Trust him."

"Have trust and die poor," Del Tacca retorted, magisterially exploiting another mainstay in the theory of barroom debate, that is, resorting to a proverb or a figure of speech, to be used, not just to grab attention, but as a lever to be inserted into the weak points of your opponent's dialectical machinery and derail his arguments. "You don't trust the doctor when he tells you you have high blood pressure, and you trust him when he tells you someone was poisoned. You remember what happened the last time we trusted a doctor?"

"It isn't that I don't trust the doctor, fathead. I don't listen to him. It's different."

"I'm sorry," Tiziana cut in, "but why—"

Here Tiziana would have liked to ask: Why use something as complicated as Tavor, when there are so many nice poisons to kill someone, especially in the middle of a conference where there are obviously lots of opportunities and lots of possible suspects? But at that moment, through the door and the rain, they caught a glimpse of a man in the blue K-Way of a municipal policeman, who immediately catalysed the attention. At least, the attention of Massimo and Aldo. Massimo glared at Aldo, while the latter dragged calmly at his cigarette as if to say: I assume full responsibility. In the meantime, the man had taken shelter from the rain under the arches and was attaching his bicycle to a lamppost.

"If that's a policeman, I'll pay the fine."

"It isn't a policeman," Aldo retorted in a reassuring tone. "I know all of them."

In the meantime, having finished anchoring his bike, the blue K-Way rubbed his hands and came into the bar.

"Hi," he said, removing his hood. He wasn't a policeman. Massimo also knew all of them. But there was something vaguely familiar about him. While Massimo was trying to think where the hell he could have seen this guy, if he really had seen him, the man took off the K-Way and Massimo's doubts vanished. With that creased orange T-shirt, the potential customer could only be the loquacious and friendly Professor A. C. J. Snijders.

"A *lungo*, please. And . . . do you have croissants?"

"They're just coming out. You did say a *lungo*?" Tiziana asked, not because she hadn't heard him but because she hadn't heard anybody order a *lungo* since 2002, when her employer had made an extremely pedantic as well as unrequested speech to an improvident Piedmontese tourist about the inherent barbarity of drinking coffee that was too diluted. Making a show of having understood, the tourist had then ordered a *ristretto* and a glass of mineral water, poured the coffee into the glass, and immediately knocked it back in one go before leaving without paying.

"Yes, please. And three croissants."

"God help us!" Ampelio said, leaning forward on his stick. "Haven't you been home yet today?"

"I beg your pardon?"

"Don't pay any attention to him," Massimo said in the hope of reasserting that the bar was his. "This three-legged old man was wondering if they were all for you. You know, people here don't mind their own business even if you kill them."

"Oh, I get it," Snijders replied, completely unfazed. "Yes, they're for me. I need to have a good breakfast. I was thinking of visiting Pisa and not stopping for lunch. It's a tourist city. That means it's expensive."

"And how are you getting to Pisa?" Pilade asked.

"With that," Snijders replied, pointing to the bike. "I hired it at the hotel."

"All the way to Pisa by bike?" Tiziana asked incredulously. "In this rain?"

"Why not? I'm not made of sugar."

"Amazing!" Ampelio said approvingly, clearly satisfied to see that, in this era of vices and perversions like traveling by car, someone still used a bicycle as a means to move around. "It's not even six miles, and flat all the way. You'll be there in half an hour."

"Half an hour. Yes, that's easy. Thank you," Snijders said, taking the first croissant. "I hope to see at least the square and the cemetery this morning. This afternoon I have to go back to the conference."

"Oh, have you come from the conference?" Ampelio asked with a knowing air. "The one where that Japanese man was killed?"

It's not possible. I don't believe it. An hour has gone by. One hour. I found out about this business an hour ago, and I swore to Fusco that I wouldn't say anything. Now my grandfather's passing the news across the Iron Curtain. I give up.

"Killed, that's right," Snijders replied, then thought for a moment. "I mean, no. Not that man. He died, yes. But it was an accident."

"In the newspaper it's an accident," Ampelio replied. "Taccini's fiancée said it was an accident too, when she became pregnant while he was a soldier in Greece. I have to say, some accidents happen if you make them happen."

"No, excuse me, I think you're mistaken," Snijders tried to argue, probably wondering all the while who Taccini was. "It was an accident. The poor old man hit his head."

"Oh, yes," Massimo said bitterly, trying to dilute his dismay in his beloved iced tea, "it's always the wrong old man who bangs his head."

"What the gentleman means," Del Tacca cut in with the politeness that the residents of Pineta reserved exclusively for strangers and those who were slow on the uptake, "is that the poor man died from respiratory arrest. A rather unusual respiratory arrest. At least so it seems."

"I don't understand," Snijders said, groping for a chair, an obvious clue that even though he didn't understand, it was his intention to stay there until some light was thrown on the matter.

"If you want to get to Pisa," Massimo said, "I think you ought to set off now. Not that I'm trying to interfere . . . "

I just want to carry on minding my own business. If Fusco finds out, he'll arrest me and put me in prison with all the rest of the retirement home. Which is why, kind and friendly professor, if you stopped asking questions and just got the hell out of here, I might still have a slim hope that all this could remain confined to the inside of this bar for the half day required before the news becomes official.

"Oh, it doesn't matter," Snijders said with a smile, glancing outside at the rain that continued unperturbed to drum on the roofs of the cars. "I don't think the Leaning Tower is made of sugar either. It should still be in the same place if I go there this evening. Could I have a cappuccino please?"

"It's quite incredible," Snijders said, playing with the crumbs of the croissants (five of them) remaining on the plate.

It had taken about twenty minutes, subdivided into two of introductions, five of actual narration, and thirteen of extra time during which the old-timers bickered with one another to make sure of the right to speak, to explain the facts—and above all what had been said about the facts—to the attentive and very curious Dutch professor. Now, while Snijders was observing how incredible it all was, Massimo was thinking more or less the same thing.

Incredible.

I attract gossips like flies. From all over Europe they come. I should start putting it on the menu. Espresso, 80 cents. Cappuccino, 1 euro. Slander of people I've never seen or known, on the house.

"Incredible, but true," Aldo said out of a sense of inertia: Snijders was silent, and since this was, after all, a bar, somebody had to say something. "Just like in one of those puzzle magazines."

"True," Del Tacca cut in. "The trouble is, even the people investigating won't get any further than the crossword. You should know, my dear Professor Sneie, that the inspector we're talking about isn't exactly on the ball."

"On the ball?"

"What Pilade means," Aldo translated, "is that the person dealing with the case is no genius."

"It depends on the moment," said Tiziana, who was now participating fully in the discussion. "Say what you like, but this time he did something clever."

"It depends on the person," Massimo said, wiping the tables with a cloth just to have something to do and trying to tell himself over and over that this was his bar, although maybe not for much longer, because if you murder your grandfather they'll arrest you, which makes running a bar a little difficult.

"If he'd told me and only me, maybe yes, that would have been clever. But to tell the official town crier of the Annoying Old Men's Cooperative doesn't strike me as a great idea. Who was the information supposed to be kept from? The people at the conference. Who's the first person you tell? A delegate to the conference. You do the math."

"Come on, Massimo, don't talk crap. How was Fusco to know that someone from the conference, someone who actually speaks Italian, would show up here today? It was an accident."

One of the most tiresome aspects of human beings is the ridiculous belief that they are not responsible for the consequences of their actions, as witness the childish casualness with which, all too often, we attribute the disastrous outcome of our stupidity to fate.

It was an accident.

It was an accident, he was coming back from a wedding and had drunk a few too many toasts, and besides what was that woman doing in the middle of the road? It was a piece of bad luck, he ate a big meal and then went for a swim to help his digestion and had a heart attack. It wasn't his fault, he simply lit a fire next to a pine grove in the middle of August.

That kind of statement really pissed Massimo off. It's all a matter of probability. If you behave in a certain way, the probability that something will go wrong increases. The fact that you didn't want to cause trouble doesn't diminish the fact that, objectively, you've caused a lot of trouble. You just have to think about it for a moment. It's why rules of safety, rules of behavior, exist. 99.9% of the time you don't need them. You only need them in the 0.1% of the time when something goes wrong. If you had kept your brain alert and stuck to the rules like a good boy, maybe nothing would have happened.

"Just shut me up, it's best for everyone."

"You don't have to worry, Massimo," Snijders said. "I don't

intend to tell anyone at the conference. I have my reasons. Now that you've told me, I need to speak to that inspector as soon as possible."

"What?" Massimo asked, while four arthritic necks, whose owners had understood perfectly well what was about to happen, turned toward the professor.

"I need to speak to him. I heard something yesterday at the conference that might be important."

Silence. Total silence. Sometimes, very rarely, there are times, some shorter, some longer, when you don't hear a single sound. The rain had stopped pouring, no car was passing along the avenue, no housewife was torturing an old tune, in other words none of the noises that constituted the normal if tiresome morning background of the bar allowed themselves to disturb the peace. It seemed as if nature had coordinated things in such a way as to have a little tranquility, because people were talking here. For a second or two Massimo savored this wonderful lack of sensation, before Snijders broke the silence by clearing his throat and launching into what showed all the signs of being a long preamble.

"Yesterday, I heard Asahara talking with a group of American professors. They were talking mainly about other people, what they were doing as research and so on. After a while, the name Watanabe was mentioned."

A pause, and a sip of cold cappuccino that made Massimo shudder just to see him take it.

"Masayoshi Watanabe is a professor in Kobe. A theoretician, like me and like Asahara. He's a well-known scientist, publishes a lot, and does things that are very, let's say, elaborate. He has at his disposal a cluster of a few thousand processors that for all intents and purposes are used only by himself and his students. He mainly does large-scale parallel simulations of the mechanical behavior of polymers and biological materials."

We haven't understood a damned thing, the faces of the old-timers said in unison. Becoming aware of this, Snijders brought his speech down to earth:

"In other words, he does some very demanding and very expensive research that uses lots of computers. I know him by sight, like Asahara, but I've had only a few opportunities to talk to him. It's no secret, though, that a lot of people in Japan don't like him. Especially Asahara, who was a theoretician of the old school and never liked Watanabe's way of doing research. The fact is, a large percentage of the funding that the Japanese government allocates for research goes to Watanabe and his center. And if it goes to him, it doesn't go to the others."

"I see," Tiziana said mistakenly. "But they didn't kill *him*."

"That's not the point. The point is that the Japanese government depends for its funding decisions on what other professors say, usually the most important ones in the country. And Asahara was a member of the advisory board. Now, what I heard was this. I heard Asahara say that there was something in his computer that would destroy Watanabe."

Ah, Massimo thought. Well, well, we have our murderer, the old-timers' faces exclaimed.

"Now, given what you've told me, I'm sure you'll agree that the first thing I should do is talk to the police."

"Oh, of course," Del Tacca said. "But phone home first. The man in charge is quite capable of arresting you for stealing your clothes from the rag merchant."

"I'm sorry?"

"No, don't say sorry," Ampelio said. "There's no point."

"Grandpa, please just shut up," Massimo cut in. "Excuse me, professor, but there's something not quite right. What words did Asahara use exactly? Did he really say destroy?"

"Oh, yes. That's what he said all right. In my laptop, he said, I have something that will destroy Professor Watanabe. He was laughing when he said it. I thought he was joking. But now . . ."

"And what do you think it could have been?" Aldo asked, in a tone that said, come on, we're not going to believe everything this scarecrow says, are we?

"I have my suspicions," Snijders replied, not even noticing the old man's doubtful attitude. "Like I said, a center doing calculations like the one Watanabe runs needs money. Lots of money. Without funding, it won't get anywhere. Now, it's possible that Asahara, being on the board that's supposed to evaluate Watanabe's funding request, was of a negative opinion. And that this opinion, in other words, his report advising against giving funding to Watanabe, or even preventing it, was on his laptop."

Snijders finished his by now ice-cold cappuccino while Massimo looked away, then resumed:

"This is just a hypothesis, of course. It needs checking. We'd need to know if it really was possible for Asahara to do that. If he was that powerful. And if the board really is due to meet soon."

"And, obviously, if a negative opinion from Asahara would really have destroyed Watanabe," Tiziana said. "Isn't that a bit drastic?"

"I've no idea," A. C. J. replied with a smile. "I don't know what you mean."

"She means that it seems a little exaggerated that an opinion could destroy a person's activities," Aldo said. "And I have to say I don't completely disagree. Not that I have any experience of these things, so I may not be the right person to judge."

"It depends," Snijders replied. "In general, you're right. But it depends. A group may be in difficulty, may have had a series of setbacks, and so is counting a lot on financing. True, it's unlikely that a failed bid for funding could lead to the destruction of the group. But it may be the beginning of the end. Maybe you have some really good young people under you, and you'd like to hold on to them, but without money and without prospects you can't. It may seem impossible. Maybe it is."

Snijders stood up, pulled up the zipper of his K-Way, and walked to the cash register to pay.

"That's five-seventy for the breakfast and six hundred for the information," Massimo said.

"I'm sorry?"

"Five-seventy. But to get to the police station, you'll have to walk five or six hundred yards through the pine grove. As soon as you leave here, you'll see a sign with the words Poseidon Bathing. Take the path just after that and go in the opposite direction from the sea. After six hundred yards, turn right and you're there."

Pilade now butted in. "Go that way and you'll get lost. Listen to me, as soon as you leave here, go straight along the street with the trees. After Caterina Bathing turn right onto the avenue where the hookers are. After two hundred yards, on your right, there's a shop that sells bicycles. Next to it is the police station."

Apart from the fact that the bathing establishment mentioned by Pilade was actually called Catalina, the directions contained one detail that seemed to escape Snijders. Sure enough, he asked for clarification.

"The avenue where what are?"

"The ladies," Rimediotti said, in a drastic attempt to save the situation by resorting to the politically correct. Unfortunately, even though salvaging the dignity of the town, Rimediotti's gloss did not make the route any more comprehensible. Fortunately, though, Aldo, who was a man of the world and knew all about illicit liaisons, stepped in.

"The kind you people put in the window."

"Oh, thank you. I think I understand now. Well, have a nice day."

"You too," Ampelio said. "If you happen to be back before one, you'll still find us all here."

FIVE

N ame and surname?" Fusco asked.
"What's your name, please?" Massimo translated.
"*O-namae wa, onegai shimasu?*" Kawaguchi asked.
"Masayoshi Watanabe."
"Masayoshi Watanabe."
"Yes, I got it. Masayoshi Watanabe."
"How do you write that?" Officer Galan asked.

It's going to be a long day, Massimo thought. Me and my big ideas.

At about 7:30 that morning, Massimo had been in the bar with Tiziana, trying to decide what to do with the day. The conference was no longer his problem: the evening before, he had received a phone call from a secretary clearly in a state of panic who had announced to him that the work of the conference had been temporarily suspended by the organizing committee "out of respect for the memory of Professor Asahara," and that this also included the suspension of the catering service for the breaks in the conference. Out of respect for the memory my ass, Massimo had thought, but had nevertheless considered it wise not to tell the secretary that he knew perfectly well how things stood. Clearly, both inside and outside the conference, there were now those who were in a position to spread the news effectively. In the meantime, though, his week's schedule had all gone to pot.

Having planned to spend his mornings and afternoons at

the conference, Massimo had asked Tiziana to come in for the whole week, on overtime pay, and so Tiziana had showed up punctually at seven to take over the bar. Punctually and pointlessly, given that Massimo no longer had any outside commitments and given that, the weather being what it was, it didn't look as if the bar was going to be doing much business anyway. Heedless of the calendar, which boldly showed the date *May 23*, the sky had decided to annoy Pineta and its inhabitants with a nice cold day, the kind of treacherous spring cold that grabs you by the ankles and calves, which are bare of socks because it's supposed to be summer, and had compounded the insult with one of those dull, persistent drizzles that seem not so much to wet you as to anoint you, not strong enough to make you take an umbrella, but just strong enough to form puddles in which, walking quickly because of the cold, you inevitably end up sooner or later. Be that as it may, since you can curse the sky as much as you want but you can't change it, what you have to change is your day's schedule, and this was what Massimo had started to discuss with Tiziana.

"If you want to rest, I can stay in the bar," Tiziana had said. "Seeing as I'm here. I think one person will be more than enough today."

"No, thanks, I don't need to rest," Massimo had said. "The fact is, I have nothing to do. I organized things so that I could work here and at the conference. Now there's nothing happening at the conference, and as for the bar, you're right, it's quite likely there'll be nobody coming in. But if I'm going to twiddle my thumbs, I prefer to do it in the bar rather than at home."

After a brief silence, a sly gleam had come into Tiziana's eyes. "Listen, Massimo," she had said, "if you really want to be here, I have a proposition to make. In the interests of the bar."

"I'm listening," Massimo had replied, wondering how likely it was that Tiziana was about to propose coming to work topless.

"I've been working here for four years, right?"

Oh, God. She wants a raise.

"Now, don't get offended, but in the four years I've been here this place hasn't changed one bit. The same walls, the same pictures, the big-screen TV over there, the tables there . . . Don't you ever get bored?"

I don't know, Massimo had thought, letting his eyes wander around the bar. I don't think so.

"Anyway, I was thinking it wouldn't be a bad thing to freshen it up a bit. Paint a couple of the walls a nice color, maybe with a sponging effect or something like that. Put up some nice reproductions or some nice photographs, put some nice curtains on the windows. Something to make the place a bit more cheerful. Don't misunderstand me, I don't mean it's dirty or badly maintained, but on a day like today anyone coming in would look at the place, see the old codgers, and wonder what time the funeral starts."

Massimo had looked around. On closer inspection, it did indeed seem that Tiziana might not be entirely wrong. The fact was, there were things that Massimo really didn't pay attention to until they were pointed out to him, and so he had never noticed the fact that the inside of the bar was starting to look a tad stale.

"So, tell me, Miss Architect," Massimo had said. "What would you change?"

"Well, it really wouldn't need much," Tiziana replied, smiling with all thirty-two of her teeth and starting to look a little overexcited. "First of all, two of the walls should be in color. I'd make one yellow, it gives a feeling of light, and one to match the counter and the floor. Of course, I'm not sure what would match that slate-gray floor, but I'll think about it. Then I'd put up three or four reproductions, I really like the ones printed directly on canvas, but the ones you get around here are crap, maybe a few nice black and white photographs would be better, something like Mapplethorpe, I don't know if you know the kind of thing I mean. One here, one there, two here, maybe a bit out of line, to give more of a sense of movement, otherwise it'll look too much like an exhibition and that wouldn't be right. Before anything else, we have to get rid of the two monstrosities hanging there, we can put a curtain or a Venetian blind over the big window, that should make us look more decent from the street. If it's O.K. with you, I'll have a look around today, and then tomorrow we're closed anyway so I can come in and arrange everything. What do you think?"

Help. I've unleashed a monster.

Massimo had again let his eyes wander around the bar before coming to rest on what Tiziana had called "the two monstrosities": a framed page from a newspaper showing the Torino soccer team, with the caption "1942-1949: Only Fate Could Beat Them," and a front-page from the *Gazzetta dello Sport*, dated December 5, 1993, announcing a record jackpot on the pools. Thanks to a biunivocal correspondence between that Sunday's results and the ones written by Massimo on the coupon, our hero had come into possession of part of that jackpot, as a result of which he had said goodbye to mathematics, his doctorate, and an uncertain future, and had bought the bar. *His* bar and nobody else's. At least, that was what he had thought at the beginning. First, it had been invaded by the veterans of the Alpine brigades, and now even Tiziana was throwing a monkey wrench in the works.

"What can I say? I don't know. I can't picture it."

"But do you like it?"

"Tiziana, I just told you I can't picture it. You sound like my grandmother, who used to ask me if I liked the soup even before I'd tasted it."

"All right, then? Will you let me do it?"

The moment of decision. To be honest, she was kind of right. Why not?

At that moment, the telephone had rung, and Massimo had gone to answer it.

"Good morning, Bar Lume."

"Hello, is that the Bar Lume?" It was the familiar voice of Officer Galan.

"Yes, it's still the Bar Lume, just as it was before. Why don't you trust me?"

A moment's silence.

"Pineta Police Station here. Inspector Fusco would like to speak with you. I'm putting you through. Please hold on."

"Hello, Signor Viviani? Am I disturbing you?"

Am I disturbing you? What's happening? Politeness, from Fusco? Come on, let's respond in kind. He deserves it.

"No, Dr. Fusco, please go ahead."

"I have an enormous favor to ask you. First, though, I need to check something. I've been told you speak English fluently. Is that right?"

What now? For a moment, Massimo had seen himself sitting at a desk, in the company of Fusco as a child in a blue smock, though already with a mustache, and reciting, "Lesson number one. Listen and repeat. The book is on the table, and the pencil is on the book."

Recovering, he replied, "Yes, it is."

"Good. Could you join me at the station? I really need you urgently. I repeat, this is a favor I'm asking. I can't force you. But—"

"Don't worry, it's no problem. I'll be right there. At least it's something to do."

Hanging up, Massimo had seen the disconsolate look on Tiziana's face: she had clearly grasped the fact that the phone call had turned her from an architect back into a barmaid.

"Do you want me to stay here?" she had said, in a voice that seemed to repaint the whole day gray.

Massimo hadn't had the heart to say yes. "No, it isn't necessary. In a while, the retirement home will be here. You can leave Aldo in charge, especially since nobody will be coming in this weather anyway."

"So can I do what I said?" she had asked, once again emboldened.

"Of course. Listen, I give you carte blanche. There are only two things I'm going to veto. No curtains or blinds. There are already people who mistake this bar for a nursing home, I don't want them to start thinking it's a brothel too. And you're not to touch what you call 'the two monstrosities.'"

"Couldn't we at least move them?"

"Maybe. But they stay on the walls. Right, I'm off. See you tomorrow, I guess."

"Yes, bwana. See you tomorrow. And thanks."

Immediately on arriving at the police station, he had been shown into the inspector's office, which contained, apart from the Representative of Law and Order himself, a man of about sixty and a slightly younger woman, blonde and very thin, who was sitting on the edge of her chair, throwing all her weight onto the balls of her feet, the muscles of her legs tensed as if she were ready to get up at any moment. The man, on the other hand, was resting against the back of his chair with his hands folded over one thigh, although the constant drumming of his index fingers betrayed a certain nervousness. Both men had gotten to their feet when Massimo entered, while the woman had remained on the starting blocks, merely turning her head in a brave but unconvincing attempt at a smile.

"Good morning, Signor Viviani," Fusco said. "Let me introduce Professor Marchi and Signora Ricciardi. The professor is the scientific organizer of the conference, and Signora Ricciardi is the head of the organizing committee."

Professor Marchi identified himself with a nod of the head

and a "Good morning" uttered in a cordial if slightly shrill voice.

"I sent for you," Fusco resumed when Massimo had sat down, "because we have a problem. As you may recall, a Japanese professor who was a guest at the conference died suddenly two days ago. Now"—Fusco was looking closely at Massimo, trying to make sure that Massimo wasn't going to let slip the fact that he already knew the whole story—"we have a problem."

"Go on," Massimo replied, reassuring Fusco with a movement of the head that he hoped was imperceptible, or incomprehensible, to the other two.

"Unfortunately, the doctor was unable to issue a death certificate. In fact, certain elements have come to light that clearly indicate that the professor's death cannot be ascribed to natural causes. All this makes it necessary to open an official investigation," Fusco said, making his voice a touch harsher on the word "necessary," as if to implicitly remind everyone in the room that he was merely doing his duty and that if chemists murdered each other at conferences it wasn't his fault.

Professor Marchi nodded to show that he had understood. "Necessary, but not painless," he said, in that shrill voice that clashed a little with his elegant and nonchalant air and his thick beard streaked with gray. "In other words, from the way things have been presented by Inspector Fusco, we realize that an investigation is necessary. And we agree with it. At the same time, we find ourselves in a difficult position. I'm sure you understand," Marchi said in the amiable tone of a person accustomed to not having to raise his voice in order to be listened to. "We're running a conference, which means implicitly that we are responsible for our guests." A pause, to let his listeners absorb the concept. "It has already been quite distressing to learn of the death of one of them. Now we are told that there is a possibility that another one may be arrested. And that disturbs us, insofar as we are, as I've said, responsible for our guests."

"Nobody mentioned any arrests," Fusco said, drumming with his pencil on the desk. "But we do find ourselves having to question people. I thought it only good manners to call you here and warn you in advance, rather than present you with a fait accompli. I'm perfectly well aware that the situation is unusual. In fact, and I beg you to believe me, from my point of view it's a disaster. To sum up the situation, I'm faced with the need to question a large number of people who are potential witnesses. Most of these people will leave the conference and Italy on Saturday, which means that I have three days to question them, because there's no way I can put two hundred people in custody, let alone force them to stay in the country. Once everyone has been questioned, I should ideally be able to establish what happened and, if there has indeed been a crime, to identify the culprit and make an arrest."

Fusco slowed down the rhythm of his drumming, looked at the two academics, then resumed:

"But let's be honest. Given the situation, and given the time limit, it's very unlikely I'll be able to discover what happened, and I don't have the slightest hope of being able to arrest anyone. What concerns me, I want to make this quite clear, is to do things as best as I possibly can and not make glaring errors. I don't want to be criticized or reprimanded as far as form goes, because, I repeat, as far as substance goes, I can't guarantee a result. On the contrary. I think I can assure you that, whatever happens, we don't have the slightest chance of obtaining a result."

Fusco put down his pencil and looked at Massimo. *God, it's down to me. I think I already got the idea, but let's hear it.*

"Now this is where we are. As I said, there isn't much time and I have to make some choices. In theory, there are 226 people I should question. Most of them don't speak Italian. For that reason, I need interpreters. I asked Police Headquarters in Pisa for help, but they flatly refused. I also approached Florence, and they may send me one person tomorrow. It's not enough. I need outside help, and I can't use any of the conference delegates, since theoretically they're all possible suspects. That's why I need you, Signor Viviani, to be my interpreter for the first part of the interviews. Are you willing to do that?"

Yes, I was right. Do I have any choice? More importantly, do I have anything else to do?

"Yes, of course."

"Good. As I was saying, we'll have to make some choices. Before anything else—"

"Excuse me, Inspector," Signora Ricciardi cut in—from her voice, Massimo recognized her as the woman who had phoned him six times a day for the whole month preceding the conference, haggling over the cost of everything and making his life a misery—"but I need you to explain something to me. Signor Viviani here"—she pointed at him with her thumb, and her voice turned acid—"also worked at the conference, serving during the coffee breaks. Why isn't he a suspect? Not that I have anything against him, let's be clear about that, I just wanted to know."

"As far as I know, Signor Viviani was not acquainted with the victim, or with anybody else present at the conference," Fusco replied, forcing himself to be patient. "In addition, Signor Viviani has already given ample proof of his usefulness to the police in a previous investigation, and his observational skills would be a great asset to me."

Take that, bitch. First he treats me kindly, and then he defends me. He's quite something today, is Fusco.

"All right, then. Now . . . " To cut things short, Fusco pressed the button on the intercom.

"Yes, sir?" Officer Galan intoned.

"Galan, we're almost ready to start. When you see the professor out, wait five minutes and then bring in the first of the witnesses." Fusco switched off the intercom. "As I was saying, we don't have much time and we'll have to make some choices. Since the victim is Japanese, we'll begin with the Japanese. There are about twenty of them. It'll be necessary to—Why are you laughing?"

"I'm sorry," Professor Marchi said, having indeed let out a little puff that had sounded like a stifled laugh. "It's just that it occurred to me you may have a few problems questioning the Japanese."

"Why?" Fusco asked, with a nervous smile. "Are they going to hit me?"

"Good heavens, no," Marchi replied. "But, you see, some of them are very old. Their English is terrible. In general, the Japanese don't speak English well. To be honest, they speak it even worse than the Italians, and you know how bad they are . . . In addition, for Japanese of a certain age, English was the language of the enemy. To be honest, in some cases you might not understand a word."

Fusco gave Massimo a questioning look. He received a positive response.

"It's true," Massimo said, "from what little I've heard, the Japanese in general are hard to understand. But if you don't mind, I'd like to suggest a solution."

"Go on."

"Among the younger Japanese, there are some who speak excellent English. I heard them during the coffee breaks. One in particular. We could ask him to work with us for the most difficult cases. It'll be like a relay. I'll translate from Italian to English, and then he'll translate from English to Japanese, and vice versa."

Fusco muttered something, then slowly began to nod. "All right. Let's do it. What's this fellow's name?"

Koichi Kawaguchi was nervous. Very nervous. Firstly, he was nervous because he liked Italian espresso very much, and had not taken into account the fact that the intensity of the flavor went hand in hand with the concentration of caffeine, which was why after three days the ration of six cups a day he'd been sticking to, apart from keeping him awake with his eyes wide open two nights in a row, was starting to give him a touch of tachycardia and hands as sweaty as sponges. Secondly, he had been summoned to the police station together with all his countrymen for some reason he was unable to ascertain, but which some maintained was connected with the death of Professor Asahara. Thirdly, they had called him aside after a while and explained to him that, in collaboration with another person, he would have to help the Italian police to question some of his colleagues who had difficulties with English. Although from one point of view this had filled him with pride, it hadn't helped to make him any calmer. In a way, singled out from his compatriots like this, he felt a bit of a traitor, even though he was aware he wasn't doing anything wrong. Last but not least, the other person was the man with a face like a Taliban fighter whom Koichi had seen first behind the counter during the coffee break, as if he were a waiter, and who was now present at the police interviews.

Putting two and two together, Koichi had become convinced that Massimo belonged to the Secret Service, and that he had been keeping some of the conference delegates under surveillance for quite a while. And this was the thing that made him most nervous of all.

"Did you know Professor Asahara?" Fusco asked, taking his eyes off Professor Watanabe and reading the prepared question from a sheet of paper.

I bet you did, Massimo thought.

Masayoshi Watanabe was a small man in his sixties, no

more than five feet tall, impeccably dressed in gray and as stiff as a pole, with a motionless, rigid, contemptuous expression, vaguely reminiscent of an Indian chief with an ulcer. His whole person gave off a mixture of moral rigor, severity, and irritation that, in spite of his ridiculous height, made you uncomfortable just to look at him.

The question was turned into English by Massimo and reformulated by Koichi in Japanese with one or two extra bows by way of punctuation. Watanabe, apparently without taking his upper teeth away from his lower teeth, replied in a kind of rapid, monotone growl composed almost exclusively of consonants, in which Massimo thought he made out the word "Asahara." Koichi carried the reply back from Kyoto to London, and Massimo accompanied it from England to Pineta:

"He says Professor Asahara had honored him with his friendship for many years, and that his death is a terrible loss to science and to all who knew him."

The interview went on like this for a while: Fusco asked his questions in an impersonal voice, Watanabe growled sentences that seemed for all the world like complicated and highly contemptuous insults, and Koichi passed on very polite and appropriate answers that Massimo translated faithfully for the inspector.

After a few minutes of this curious wireless telephone, Fusco said, "On the first day of the conference, the victim referred to the contents of his computer, saying with a great deal of certainty that the said contents would be able to destroy you. This has been ascertained thanks to the statement of a witness. I quote verbatim the statement of Professor Antonius Snijders: 'In my laptop, I have something that will destroy Professor Watanabe.' Do you recall these words?"

"No," Massimo said after the usual interlude, noting that Watanabe's face was becoming even stiffer.

"Would you care to speculate as to what these particular

contents could have been, or what subject they might have concerned?"

"No," Massimo repeated, trusting to Koichi, but unable to help noticing that the "no" uttered by Watanabe the second time, while definitively negative in substance, had seemed a little clearer and longer in form than the previous one.

"Given the circumstances, I must ask you if you have ever had any reason to wish for the death of Professor Asahara."

Massimo translated, and Koichi looked at him over his glasses with a worried air. Don't make me ask this question, his nervous face said in Esperanto. There was a moment of embarrassed silence, made all the heavier by the fact that, as far as Massimo could tell, Watanabe had understood the question perfectly well.

"Please translate," Fusco said, somewhat impatiently.

"*Watanabe gakucho* . . . " Koichi began, bowing as low as a skier, but was silenced by Watanabe with what amounted to an order, curt and peremptory, uttered in an English as bad as it was threatening:

"No nid transration!"

There was indeed no need of translation. Either of the question, or of the answer.

In the two minutes that followed, according to what Koichi, still bowing like an oscilloscope, passed on to Massimo, a volcano in the shape of Watanabe explained, in a tone that overcame all language barriers, the many ways in which this question offended him, as a professor and as a Japanese, concluding that he had already being insulted enough that morning and that he had no intention of answering any more stupid questions. With this, the acute phase of the eruption being over, the Japanese luminary turned and left the room without even closing the door behind him, leaving the heterogeneous quartet of inquisitors in a state of visible embarrassment.

"Frankly, I'd have preferred it if he'd tried to hit me," Fusco said in a tone of forced indifference after a few seconds, without waiting for Massimo's translation. "Galan, since the door's already open, go get the next one, and God help us!"

The following witness, according to Fusco's schedule and as confirmed vocally by the person himself, was Dr. Shin-Ichi Kubo, in other words one of Asahara's three close colleagues at the conference, being a member of the same department as the dead man. The thirty-five-year-old Kubo, too, was impeccably dressed in gray, but unlike Watanabe (apart from being taller than a night table), did not keep his eyes fixed on Fusco but stared down at the floor, as if he did not have the strength to look up. It was obvious, though, from the bags under his eyes and his hangdog look, that Asahara's death had been a terrible blow to him. He too was asked the ritual questions, which he answered simply, still looking at the floor as if reading the answers from the tiles. Of course he knew Professor Asahara: he had been a colleague of his for three years, ever since he had moved to Waseda, the university in Tokyo where he worked. No, he didn't know that the professor had had myasthenia. No, Asahara did not suffer from depression, or at least had never shown any signs of it. Yes, he knew that Asahara had said those words: they had been reported to him by another colleague, Goro Kimura. He had not heard them himself, because he had not been present at the morning coffee break: since he was supposed to be giving rather an important presentation on Wednesday, he had stayed in the conference hall with his laptop during all of the coffee breaks, finishing his presentation and going over it. No, he didn't know what Professor Asahara had been referring to when he had said those words.

"Now, Dr. Kubo," Fusco said, with a hint of kindness that struck Massimo, "I must ask you to make one last effort to cooperate. We have here Professor Asahara's laptop, which we got from his room. At this point, given the scarcity of clues, we have to analyze its contents. We need a person who knew the dead man and who can help us to analyze them, in the presence of our experts."

Here, Fusco was downplaying the fact that the large, efficient group of people suggested by the term "our experts" consisted, sadly, of a single person, Officer Turturro, who had joined the police after two years studying computer engineering.

Having said this, Fusco leaned down and picked up a case from which he extracted a brand-new laptop, which he placed on the desk while Massimo and Koichi were translating. Kubo listened to Koichi's translation with a frown, and after looking at the laptop turned in surprise to Koichi and quickly said something. Before the translation arrived, Massimo had the feeling that he already knew what he would have to tell Fusco, and, unusually, the feeling turned out to be accurate.

"He says this isn't the late Professor Asahara's computer."

Fusco gave him a sidelong look. "How can he say that? We took it from the dead man's room. Of course it's his."

After a brief Italo-Anglo-Japanese exchange, which didn't actually seem necessary given that Kubo seemed to understand the questions perfectly well in English, Massimo was able to give a more comprehensive explanation:

"Dr. Kubo says this isn't the laptop he always saw Asahara work on, which he brought with him to Italy. This one is a different model."

"I understand. But I don't see why this one couldn't also be his. We found it in his room. I know there are sometimes thefts from hotel rooms. But those are thefts, not swaps. We can try turning it on anyway, and seeing what's in it. If this computer was the dead man's, Dr. Kubo here might be able to recognize the contents."

There followed a medium-length exchange.

"Dr. Kubo says we can try, and that if the computer is Asahara's, it can easily be ascertained. Apparently, the professor always used the same password for every computer he had access to, and Dr. Kubo, just like all the other members of the group, knows it. But he still maintains that Professor Asahara usually worked on another laptop, the one he referred to before, and that he probably meant that one when he spoke those words during the coffee break. He says that if you haven't found it, it means it's been taken."

"I understand, I understand," Fusco replied. "I'd already gotten there myself. I know perfectly well what it means if there was another laptop and we haven't found it. We'll look for it. As if this whole mess wasn't already complicated enough, all we needed was for someone to steal the computer. In the meantime, though, we have this one, and that's what we have to start with. Will you at least give me the satisfaction of switching it on and seeing if we find anything?"

Fusco wasn't completely wrong. Massimo waited a few moments, then, given that for some mysterious reason everybody seemed to be expecting him to be the one to switch on the computer, he took it, opened it, and pressed the *on* button. The object reacted with an irritable beep, then started humming softly while strings of tiny characters appeared one after another on the screen, so quickly as to make any attempt to read them impossible.

While the laptop completed its reawakening, Massimo helped Kubo to describe to Fusco the model and make of the missing computer. Then, going back to the computer screen, he saw a message in English stating that the machine was unable to start correctly, implicitly accusing the user of not having provided it with all the drivers necessary for it to work, and suggesting to the user that he should look into this and do something about it, because—this wasn't written, but could easily be inferred between the lines—if it didn't work, this was certainly not the fault of the machine.

"Something wrong?" Fusco asked, seeing that Massimo had started beating the space bar convulsively, as he always did at home when his computer refused to cooperate.

"It won't turn on."

"What?"

"It won't turn on. Or rather, it turns on but the operating system won't start. You see?" Massimo pointed at the screen, on which the obtuse device continued to maintain that it was completely unable to do anything.

"Yes, I see. But what does it mean?"

"Err . . . " Massimo said, suppressing the instinct to say, I haven't a clue what it means. "There's something that isn't working. But I don't understand what. It seems there are some internal conflicts, that some drivers are missing. There could be several reasons for that. For example . . . "

"I know, I know," Fusco said with the embittered air of someone for whom nothing ever works, no matter how hard he tries, "these things stop working when they feel like it and without any apparent reason. Look, let's finish questioning this fellow and then we'll call Officer Turturro and he can take a look at it."

The interview had concluded according to the ritual: Fusco had asked Kubo when he was planning to leave Italy, and Kubo had replied that he would be leaving on Saturday, immediately after the end of the conference, but that his colleagues in the research group, Komatsu and Saito, had planned to stay in Tuscany on vacation for the whole of the next week. Asahara was supposed to have gone back with Kubo on Saturday. After a handshake, Dr. Kubo was allowed to go and Fusco sat down again on his armchair with casters.

"Great," he said in a dejected tone. "The next one will probably tell me that the dead man wasn't a professor but a professional actor, and that the whole thing was a joke. At least, that's what I'm hoping. All right, let's get on with this farce. Galan, the next one, please."

The first round of interviews having been completed, Massimo was on his way back to the bar to have something to eat before resuming the process. A process that, apart from Watanabe's spectacular outburst, had proved distinctly monotonous. All the other Japanese interviewed, while demonstrating their eagerness to cooperate, had almost invariably answered Fusco's questions with the same sentence. Something that more or less began with "*gomennasai*" and basically meant, "I'm really sorry, but I don't know a damn thing." All of them. Well, at least this time, none of it was my fault. Now, let's have a nice *schiacciata*, and then back to doing Our Duty. And, with this thought, he entered the bar. Inside which, the only person to greet him, sadly, was Aldo, who was playing absentmindedly with a pack of cards.

"Hi, Aldo."

"Oh, it's you. No need to rush. It's only one-thirty."

"My God, you're tetchy. I'm making myself a *schiacciata*. Is the rest of the battalion at lunch?"

"Only too right. Yes, they all answered the call of their stomachs. And poor Aldo was left here to cast spells."

As he spoke, Aldo put down the pack and cut it two or three times with one hand. Then he took three cards from the pack and showed them to Massimo. Two jacks and an ace. Smiling, he took two cards between the fingers of his right hand and one in his left, holding them between thumb and middle finger; and with a slow, elegant gesture, after making sure that Massimo was watching, slid them facedown onto the table. Having done this, he looked at Massimo and pointed to the cards.

Far too easy, Massimo thought. He moved with all the speed of a sick sloth. The ace is the one in the middle.

Much less gracefully than Aldo, he picked up the card in the middle and turned it over.

Jack of spades.

Massimo stared openmouthed. He knew, because his grandfather had told him, that Aldo could do fantastic things with cards, but he had never seen him in action. Aldo looked at him and smiled smugly while Massimo turned down the volume on his iPod.

"How did you learn?"

"When I was a young man," Aldo said, "I worked as a waiter on ocean liners." He picked up the rest of the pack and started thumbing through it. "You can't imagine how bored a person can get on a ship. You have to find a way to pass the time. But, as you can imagine, there weren't many pastimes accessible to the crew, and they had to be small and cheap. And don't even think about fraternizing with the passengers."

At the word "fraternizing," Massimo's mental projector started showing a dream sequence of a young heiress, her smile a mixture of the girlish and the wanton, secretly passing the key of her cabin to Aldo wrapped inside a napkin, but he immediately shook himself out of it. Maybe I should start going out with girls again, instead of just thinking about them, he told himself while Aldo continued with his story.

"That's why, since there was no chance of learning the double bass, and I really wasn't attracted to the idea of taking it in the ass from the rest of the crew"—with these words Aldo destroyed the romantic aura in which Massimo had begun to bathe the scene—"I started learning card tricks. I'd spend hours in front of the mirror, trying over and over, without thinking about anything else. It was a hypnotic exercise, which required concentration. You really had to focus. You couldn't think about anything else. And you immediately realized that you absolutely couldn't cheat yourself. If a trick didn't look right in the mirror, if the corner of the card stuck out even for a second, you immediately realized that you couldn't try doing that trick in public. It'd come out wrong and you'd end up with egg on your face. A magician has to be infallible, otherwise he's either laughable or embarrassing."

Aldo put the cards back in their box and placed it on the table.

"Sometimes I think that all that time in front of the mirror with the cards saved my mental health. I saw people literally go crazy." Aldo was silent for a moment, then went on in a changed tone, "Now, with my arthritis I can't do most of the moves so well, but three-card monte is something I'm still pretty good at. Have you figured out what I did yet?"

"No. And I'd like to get there by myself, so don't tell me. You put the cards down one after the other. Very slowly. Did you really have an ace in your hand, or did you replace it before doing the trick?"

"That's a very good question," Aldo said, and turned over the first card on his left. "No, the ace is here."

"Right. So you put down the ace, pretending it was a jack."

"Correct. Very good."

"Oh, yes, very good. I still don't know how the hell you did it."

"Look." Aldo took the jack between the thumb and middle finger of his right hand, and the ace between the thumb and index finger of the same hand. Then he turned his hand, holding the cards facedown in such a way that the ace was over the jack, but slightly out of line with it.

"Now, I put down just these two cards. You watch me and you unconsciously take it for granted that I'm putting the lower card down first. But I'm not. Look. First I put down on the left the card that's on top, which is the ace. As soon as I've put the card down, I place my index finger, which is now free, on the edge of the card that's still in my hand, and lift my middle finger. So you'll have the impression that the card I have in my hand is the one that was underneath, which according to you I kept from the start between my thumb and my index finger. But you're wrong. At this point, very slowly and also a little bit clumsily, so that you think I've made a mess of things, I put down the second card, and the trick's done."

And he repeated the gesture very slowly, in such a way that Massimo could understand. Then he put the cards back in the pack.

"The important thing is to divert your attention, to make you believe what I want you to believe. I've seen people in ports make a decent living with this trick. And I was as good as them. Maybe better."

"I get it. But what if I pick the right card?"

"You won't. Trust me."

"I wouldn't dream of it. Trust!" Massimo made a gesture to underline the concept. "The last person I trusted was my wife, and she cheated on me. The only thing I trust is what I see."

"All right, then. You see, if we were in a port, I'd have an accomplice hidden in the crowd. If you picked the right card, I'd ask you if you felt confident enough to double the bet. And you'd probably be a bit taken aback for a moment. Just long enough for my accomplice to shout out 'I'll double the bet!' Then he'd take your place, win instead of you, and give me back the money later."

"And what if I got in first and immediately said, 'O.K., I'll double the bet'?"

"No problem. You'd win. At which point, my accomplice would sneak closer to you and once you'd walked away he'd follow you home, waiting for you to turn onto a poorly-lit street. Then he'd pull out a big club and persuade you to give him everything you have in your pocket. Of course he might beat you with the club first. Depends on the kind of person."

"I get it. But what if—"

"What if, what if. It's all bullshit, Massimo. If my grandfather had had wheels he'd have been a wagon. Get a move on, make that *schiacciata* and eat it, and then you can tell me what's going on at the police station. I've been here all morning, I think I have a right to get the news before everyone else."

SIX

T he morning of a fine day, after days of rain and wind, always puts people in a good mood. The air is crystal clear, purged of all its nanoscopic impurities, and it goes easily into your lungs, without any effort, giving you a wonderful feeling of convalescence. In the distance, you can see the mountains in all their detail, no longer obscured by the blanket of dust and smog that usually infects the atmosphere, and the town itself is clearer, better defined, more real.

All these things—the weather, the renewed ability to breathe, having something to do—had raised Massimo's mood to such a level that not even the prospect of driving to Pisa in his car had managed to piss him off as it would normally have done quite automatically.

Frightened at the prospect that the Pisan motorist might be getting lazy, the diligent workers in the traffic department had created a veritable parallel city, a kind of perverse labyrinth of no-entry signs, absurd roundabouts, and Dantesque bottle-necks. This parallel city was in turn inhabited by parallel citizens, the motorists: temporary avatars of flesh and blood, imprisoned in their cars, which were themselves hemmed in by the unavoidable density of the urban traffic, they exclusively showed the Mr. Hyde aspect of their personalities, becoming incensed at whatever happened, both inside and outside their vehicles.

The feeling Massimo sometimes had, driving inside this heap of confusion, was that the authorities had never had the intention of producing a street network but rather a mini-golf course. Yellow lines for cycle lanes and rows of retroreflectors marked off your route; cheerful blocks of white and red plastic, arranged to imitate a roundabout, forced you to overtake or slow down in the stupidest way; broad avenues fed into narrow medieval streets filled with arches, at the end of which, if you were lucky, a single free parking space awaited you so that you could at last get out of your car. But in spite of all this, Massimo was in an excellent mood. The fact that he was being forced to sacrifice part of his free day trying to figure out what was in Asahara's computer didn't bother him in the slightest. On the contrary.

The previous day, the computer had been identified by Katsuo Komatsu, another of Asahara's colleagues, as the professor's new laptop, which he had owned for only a few days. After registering the fact that the computer wouldn't turn on, Massimo had suggested a drastic solution to Fusco: that they open up the computer and read the hard disk directly through another computer. Fusco had approved of the idea, and had asked Officer Turturro if the police station had at its disposal everything required to perform this operation. Turturro had explained that it didn't, that it had practically nothing that was required, and that in any case he himself had never performed an operation of that kind on a laptop. At this point, while Fusco was looking at poor Turturro as if suspecting him of having sabotaged the computer himself, Massimo had ventured a suggestion:

"I know someone who may be able to read the hard disk. He's a technician at the University. He's very good, and he's very discreet."

"Uh-huh," Fusco said without much enthusiasm.

"If you have another solution . . . "

"Oh, no. It's just that everything here works through friends. Through official channels, nothing ever works. You're always asking, asking, asking. We don't have computers, we don't have cars, we don't have a damned thing. It's best if you don't get me started on this. Let's do as you say, Signor Viviani. All I ask is that Officer Turturro be present. I know this investigation is a complete mess, but I think I should keep it at least a little bit official."

And so Massimo and Officer Turturro had agreed to meet in Pisa the following day at the place where this person worked. That was why Massimo was now in Pisa instead of being by the sea with a towel, a book, and a sandwich, enjoying a little peace and quiet.

After avoiding all the various traps the traffic department had scattered along the route, Massimo crossed the Ponte Solferino, parked on Via Fermi, and walked to Via Risorgimento where the Department of Chemistry and Industrial Chemistry stood, or rather, endured: a sad building in retro-Fascist style, too recent to exercise the charm of long-standing university departments and too old to still be able to function decently. Looked at from the outside, it seemed to be wondering what it was still doing there. Fortunately, however, the authorities had not left the old department alone: on the other side of the street, the venerable orthopedic department of Santa Chiara Hospital kept it company and supported it in its daily battle against the beautiful and the modern.

Officer Turturro was waiting for him in the doorway of the department with the laptop case in his hand.

"Hi. Nice day, isn't it?"

"Yes, it is. Shall we go in?"

Massimo opened the door and went in, followed by Turturro, to be greeted by a terrible smell of garbage in brine that grabbed him by the stomach and accompanied him all the way to the porter's lodge. The porter did not seem remotely bothered by the aroma.

"What can I do for you?"

"Good morning. I'm looking for Carlo Pittaluga." And maybe also a bathroom. Because in two seconds I'm going to throw up.

"Who shall I say?"

"Massimo Viviani and . . . " Massimo stopped, realising that he didn't know how to introduce his companion. Officer Turturro? Signor Turturro? My personal bodyguard?

"Turturro," the officer told the porter.

"Just a moment," the porter replied, and dialed a number on his phone. "Dr. Pittaluga? Viviani and Turturro are here for you. Shall I send them up? O.K." He put down the receiver. "He says to wait here and he'll be right down."

"Thanks."

"Did you study here, signore?" Turturro asked Massimo.

"No. I studied mathematics. On Via Buonarroti. And you don't have to call me signore. Do I seem that old?"

"I did engineering. On Via Diotisalvi, over there." He made a sign with his hand, as if to underline the fact that this smell didn't reach Via Diotisalvi. "I was there for two years. Lots of theory and no practice." He smiled. "It wasn't for me."

Massimo nodded, but said nothing in reply. Partly because he wanted to avoid breathing as much as possible, partly because situations like waiting in the company of someone you hardly knew always made him feel a little uncomfortable. He realized he must seem impolite not to say anything, but on the other hand, once they had established that it was a nice day, what else was there to say? In addition, Officer Turturro struck him as the typical idiot who enrolled on an engineering course without having much idea what it involved, and who, having realised that it wasn't enough to just fiddle around with computers, but that you also needed to study and understand things in order to pass exams, dropped out, justifying his decision by saying that he was a practical person, that he wanted to do things and didn't need to study all that pointless stuff, and so on. Massimo didn't like people like that. Actually, Massimo thought, there weren't many people he did like. Fortunately, he now heard the sound of heavy but enthusiastic footsteps on the stairs and realized that Carlo had arrived. He turned, and saw the fellow descend the last steps and come toward him at a solemn pace.

Carlo Pittaluga began with a pair of size fourteen tennis shoes and ended, six and a half feet above them, in a big smile involving all thirty-two teeth, topped by two disturbingly alert green eyes. In the middle, a tartan shirt and a pair of pants appropriate to his size. Apart from belonging to the restricted number of human beings whom Massimo liked, Carlo was absolutely one of the most intelligent people he knew. Having graduated with honors, he had remained in the Chemistry Department as a graduate technician, even though, given his résumé and his skills, he would probably have been able to get a better position. Be that as it may, he was now the computer technician for the department's center for calculations, a role he fulfilled in an erratic but highly competent fashion.

"Hello, Viviani," he said, waving to Massimo as he approached.

"Hello, Pittaluga," Massimo replied with a smile. "This is Officer Turturro. What Officer Turturro is holding in his hand is the laptop I was telling you about."

"All right. Let's go straight to the computer room and read the disk. Then we'll go to my office and copy it onto a memory stick or a CD." And he headed up the stairs, followed by Massimo and Turturro.

"Does it always smell like this?" Turturro asked as they climbed the stairs.

"No, someone must have opened a fridge down in Organics. Judging by the hint of excrement, I'd guess it was Cognetti's fridge. Anyway, it's not so bad," he asserted, while the color of Massimo's face expressed the opposite opinion. "It would have been worse if they'd opened Crudeli's fridge."

"Why, what's in Crudeli's fridge?" Massimo asked. "Poison?"

"Insect pheromones. Synthesized sexual attractors for different kinds of insects."

"Are they dangerous?"

"Well, for example, three years ago one of the phials got broken, and I guess they must have synthesized those pheromones well, because within a day the department was full of bees. They were everywhere, in the air conditioning, the drawers, other places too. There were people who didn't use the toilets for weeks after that. But anyway, the smells don't get in here so much," Carlo said, stopping in front of a reinforced door and opening it with a few turns of his key. "*Et voilà.* Please come in, grab a seat."

Following Carlo, Massimo and the officer entered what was probably the most chaotic room in Europe. Beyond a glass door, about a hundred computers of various shapes and sizes were humming, filling the air with a heavy background noise. Dozens of colored wires ran all over the dimly lit room, on the floors, on the walls and around the tables, on which lay a number of disemboweled computers, with what had once been their internal components scattered here and there.

"So," Carlo said, moving a fan from a stool and bravely sitting on the latter. "Tell me what's going on. Let me make a bit of space on the desk here." With a sweep of his hand he shifted a few assorted parts, which would have fallen straight to the floor and smashed had Turturro not grabbed them. "Just stick them on the floor, they're only rubbish. O.K., now let's see how we can open this baby."

Carlo turned the computer over and started unscrewing the back with a screwdriver. As he did so, he asked Massimo, "You did tell me this thing belonged to a Japanese?"

"Yes."

"Strange."

"Why strange?"

"Because the Japanese usually have tiny laptops. Something you can hold in your hand, or even smaller. This one's big. Well, all the better. Easier to work with. Apart from anything else, I've never seen this model before. It's one of those assembled ones, I think. You see, it isn't a single block." Carlo put one of his big fingers inside the body of the laptop and used it as a lever. With a noise of something breaking, a small block no larger than a pack of cigarettes (a unit of measurement that's very useful in describing technological objects about which we know nothing, apart from the size) sprang free of the casing. "Oh, that's nice. What just came off is the hard disk. Now we'll connect it and transfer everything to Argo."

"To what?"

"To Argo," Carlo repeated, pointing to the electronic monster humming beyond the glass door.

"Argo? You mean that's one computer?"

"No, it's a lot of machines working in parallel, run by a main server that directs the processes. The server works on Mosix and is only responsible for distribution to the afferent machines," Carlo explained proudly as he connected the disk to a cable emerging from some unspecified place inside the beast, "whereas the slave multiprocessors are the real calculating machines. Each one works by itself on a specific process. We could also get them all working in parallel on a single process, but that can be a mess because of redirection."

"Yes . . . " Turturro said as if he had actually understood any of this. But what exactly are all these computers for?"

"For making calculations."

"All of them?"

"There aren't that many," Carlo said. "Chemical calculations can be really huge. A dynamic simulation or the optimization and calculation of the frequencies of a complex of a transition

metal usually takes weeks. Even if you use four or eight processors in parallel. The more processors you use, the less time it
takes. Anyway, this has almost finished copying. There wasn't
much there, as it happened. Does that make sense?"

"Yes," Turturro said. "The computer was almost new."

"Right. Now, let's go up and I'll transfer it somewhere. Do
you have anything to put it on?"

Officer Turturro nodded and took a CD from his bag.
Carlo took it delicately in his big fingers and nodded, then
relieved the stool of his weight and walked silently out of the
room, followed by the representative of the law and the representative of curiosity.

Carlo's office was no more chaotic than the computer room,
but could certainly have honourably competed with it in
untidiness. Here, Carlo copied the data, recalling it from Argo
and mastering it onto CD. Once the operation was over, he had
looked at Massimo, his eyes bursting with curiosity.

"Do you want to see what's in it right away?" Translation: if
you look at it right away you're going to send me out of the
room, aren't you?

Massimo and Turturro looked at each other. It's not up to
me, Massimo thought, but . . .

Turturro raised his eyebrows, in a gesture that could easily
have been interpreted as "I don't see any harm." Turturro's
eyebrows had not even reached their destination before Carlo
clicked twice on the first of the two folders.

"Ah, here we are. There are two documents. This is the first
one: 'Natsu,' dated May 20 at 23:21."

The first document appeared on the screen, and this time
all three raised their eyebrows.

The document, obviously, was in Japanese.

"Does either of you know Japanese?" Carlo asked.

Sitting in the car, with the windows down to enjoy the warm wind produced by the moving vehicle, Massimo's body was heading for the cash and carry in order to stock up both the bar and his home refrigerator. Massimo's brain, on the other hand, was still in Carlo's office, thinking about what they had found in Asahara's new computer. And, as always, to be sure of not losing anything of what he was thinking, Massimo was talking to himself:

"So, let's go over this. There are two folders in the computer. The first contains two documents written in Japanese. Nobody can understand a damn word because they're written in ideograms, but to judge by the look of them, they don't seem to be official documents. There are also words written in different colors. Presumably notes. Notes about what, I don't know. But clearly written for personal use. In the other folder, there's a program written in Fortran with its various input and output files. A calculation code. Carlo says it's a program for molecular dynamics. And that it's very simple. It doesn't have any peculiarity. And when it comes to such things, I trust Carlo. So whatever that old Japanese professor was referring to has to be in the documents in Japanese. And at this point, until we find a way to understand what's in them, it's best not to think about it. Turn it whichever way you want, that's the way it is. If you don't have reliable data about something, you can't start to argue about it, just as you feel. Unless you're the Pope, of course. Am I the Pope? No, for the moment I'm not. So let's go and do the shopping and not think about it anymore. This afternoon Fusco can get some random Japanese to read the documents, there are plenty of them around, and then we'll see."

Leaving the cash and carry, Massimo headed for home, in San Martino, to put his personal shopping in the fridge. Having got to Via San Martino, he should, in theory, have been able to turn under the arch in Vicolo Rosselmini and come out on Piazza San Bernardino, where he would have been able to park comfortably and drop his shopping at home, in the very same square. That was the theory. In reality, though, some idiot had parked his stupid scooter right in the middle of the arch, next to the terracotta flower beds of the restaurant, which already made it difficult enough to enter the alley without scratching the bumper. Cursing, Massimo got out of the car and tried to shift the motionless vehicle from under the arch.

Unfortunately, partly because the scooter stubbornly obeyed the laws of gravity, partly because our hero was objectively unendowed with the appropriate physical attributes, all that Massimo managed to obtain was a terrible sweat and a replenishment of his already large curriculum of blasphemies. There was no way: the scooter could not be moved. Still cursing, Massimo got back in his car, sat down on the edge of the seat in order not to touch it with his sweat-soaked back, and started to look for a parking spot, which he did not find until he got to Piazza dei Facchini, in other words, a considerable distance away. Then, as laden with bags as a llama, he headed laboriously for home.

Sometimes, when you're feeling pissed off, there's nothing better than to buy yourself something. Anything, even something stupid, in fact, preferably something stupid: something that doesn't cost much, that's absolutely superfluous, and whose sole purpose is to give you satisfaction. You see something, you want it, you go in and get it. Outside shopping, that doesn't happen often in life.

That was why, half an hour later, having finished transferring his purchases, and feeling cleansed at least in body by a nice shower, Massimo was wandering around a bookstore in search of something to keep him company on the beach and get rid of his bad mood. After hovering a long time around the mystery section and resisting the blandishments of the latest arrivals, he started to leaf through the classics. Camus, *The Myth of Sisyphus*. Must be good. Of course, Camus on a beach is like giving a piece of *pandoro* to a cat. Maybe this winter? Robbe-Grillet, *Jealousy*. Oh, please. Soseki, *I Am a Cat*. Hmm, maybe. It's certainly long. My God, what a brick. No, no, something less bulky. Roald Dahl, *Tales of the Unexpected*. Short stories. Perfect. Never read anything by this guy, but I seem to remember hearing that he's good.

Pleased with his choice, Massimo went to pay, and as he was handing the book to the cashier, he found himself thinking again about that damned scooter. Almost simultaneously, among the books displayed by the cash register he saw one that, somehow, grabbed his attention. He smiled, picked it up, placed it resolutely on the cash register next to the Dahl, and took out his wallet. The cashier, who knew him, gave him a surprised look and said, "*Three Meters Above Heaven*, by Federico Moccia. Is it a gift?"

"No, it's for me."

"Do you read this stuff?"

"I have no intention of reading it. I'm buying it as a homage to the author. It's just given me an idea."

Leaving the bookstore, Massimo walked fifty yards and went into Signor Tellini's store. He nodded in greeting, went to the counter and made a request. As usual, Signor Tellini replied with another question: a further request for clarification, to identify exactly what the customer wants, made in the tranquil tone of someone who knows that he has what you need. Having asked the question, Signor Tellini withdrew to the back room and immediately came out again with the object that Massimo had in mind. Having put the object on the counter, he explained to Massimo how it worked, both to make sure that the mechanism did not have any problems and to show him those little flaws—you have to force it a little bit like this the first few times, but then it'll run by itself, you'll see—that every mechanical device has, the secret of which has been known to him for a long time. As he was paying, Massimo asked Signor Tellini for a pen and a piece of paper, on which he wrote a brief message.

On his way home, he saw that the scooter was still in its place, and he walked quickly towards it. Then, having quickly looked around to make sure nobody was about, he did what he had to do.

Two minutes later, having completed his task, he walked rapidly and indifferently away without lingering to look. Before leaving, however, he had taken out the piece of paper with the message he had written in the store and attached it with a pin to the seat of the scooter.

On the paper, in the hated elementary school handwriting from which Massimo was unable to free himself, was written the following message:

"Dear idiot,

"Thanks to your scooter being parked in such a stupid way, I wasn't able to get through in my car. That's why I had to go and park in the back of beyond and carry my shopping bags all the way home in the sun, which was a real drag.

"As you can see, there's now a nice chain around the front wheel of your scooter. In order to take it off, so that you can then go and splatter yourself all over some wall while attempting to ride on one wheel, the best thing to do is to open it with its key. Where is the key? you must be wondering. Don't worry, I haven't taken it with me. The key is in the earth in one of the vases of flowers in front of the restaurant. I won't tell you which one in order not to spoil your fun. Hoping it's as much of a drag for you to to find it as it was for me to get home, I wish you a crappy day and sign myself your very affectionate Batman."

SEVEN

It was about seven in the evening. While in the sky the orange was just starting its ephemeral conquest of blue, somewhere further down Massimo was returning to Pineta after a day by the sea that had, objectively speaking, been thrown away.

Firstly, the sea was still too cold to bathe in. Secondly, given that it had rained during the previous few days, the sand was still too wet to have the right texture when it settled, all warm and compact, around the curves and corners of your retired accountant's physique, which meant that the idea of having a nap had turned out to be a not very inviting one.

Thirdly, taking a book of short stories to the sea had not been a wise choice. Not that they were bad. On the contrary, one or two of them were really brilliant. The fact was, it was hard for Massimo to like short stories. The constant change of atmosphere didn't involve him, or help him to identify, or even to imagine the faces of the characters. In short, they didn't produce the effect of isolation from reality that he looked for in a book. Of course, it's only natural to wonder why he had bought a book of short stories knowing that he probably wouldn't like it. Unfortunately, there is no way to know the precise reason. Each of us has a twisted way of using the bookstore of our own knowledge.

It is a fact that men with a strong sense of curiosity often feel the need to shake off their own experience, perceiving it more as a rigid shell of habit that limits movement than as a friendly protective coating, a necessary armor against the forces of the unknown. When we challenge our own habits, we are fully aware that the likelihood of victory is remote, and it is precisely the exceptional nature of such a victory that swells the victorious chest with satisfaction and wraps it in an aura of heroism on the rare occasions when we manage to cheat routine.

However, since this is a story without pretensions, it's time to put Man with a capital letter back among the dusty tomes of philosophy and focus again on man with a small *m*, an average car, and a huge nose. Massimo, in fact. As we were saying, what the traffic had been unable to do had been achieved by a not very successful day by the sea: it seemed to Massimo that he had wasted an afternoon, and when Massimo wasted time he tended to feel really pissed off.

On his way back to Pineta, he searched for a while on the radio for a song that would cheer him up, but given that the gods obviously had it in for him today, the most interesting thing he managed to pick up was a program on Radio 24 about variable-tax mortgages. At this point he gave up, switched off the radio, and started to think about his own things.

When he got to Pineta, he parked and headed for the bar, which was closed but with the shutters still up, although behind them inside the Venetian blinds were down. Massimo approached, glanced in through the cracks in the blinds, and stood there, looking into the bar. His bar. Or at least, what he had been convinced was his bar. Because his bar didn't have orange walls. Or posters. And when had it ever had Venetian blinds?

At that moment, inside the bar, the telephone rang.

Massimo unlocked the glass door and found himself confronted with an impassable barrier of wooden sticks. Cursing, he picked up an armful of sticks as best he could and created a gap to pass through, while the telephone, oblivious to the complexity of the maneuver, kept on ringing. Having got out of the tangle, Massimo made a dash for the phone, picked it up, and said, "Hello?"

"Hello, is that the Bar Lume?" said a voice with a Venetian accent.

"One moment, please."

Massimo went to the blinds, and since they were now on the inside, he pulled them up in the prescribed manner with the little rope, and went outside. He read the sign over the bar, came back in, and returned to the telephone.

"Yes, this is the Bar Lume. I'm sorry, I was starting to have my doubts. Go ahead."

"Pineta Police Station here," said the voice of Officer Galan. "Please hold on."

"Signor Viviani?" came Fusco's voice after a moment.

"Speaking."

"I've been looking for you all afternoon. Where the hell were you?"

Mind your own business, why don't you? But then he is a police inspector. Must be some kind of professional deformation.

"I was by the sea. Today was my day off."

"Listen, you're currently helping us with our inquiries into the death of Professor Asahara. You really need to remain as available as possible. Don't you have a cell phone number so that we can reach you?"

"No. I don't have a number and I don't have a cell phone. You know how it is, I really like my privacy."

There was a moment's silence.

"All right. You're the boss. But what I most care about is my work. And today you were important for my work. That's why I must ask you to be where we can reach you at all times. It's vital that you remain available. For an intelligent person like you, that shouldn't be hard to understand."

"Of course not."

"Now let's get to the point. This morning you went with Officer Turturro to the University, to see Dr. Pittaluga, who undertook to read the hard drive in Professor Asahara's laptop. In his report, Dr. Pittaluga maintains that, apart from the system folders required for the machine to work, there were only two folders in the computer. In the first there was a very simple calculation code, probably for teaching purposes according to Pittaluga. In the second there were two files. Can you confirm that there was nothing else in the computer?"

"As far as I can see, there wasn't."

"Isn't it possible that the Professor kept some files hidden in the system folders, where nobody would look for them?"

"It's possible, but extremely unlikely. Nobody of sound mind would do that."

Oh, great, I've just called him crazy.

"Yes, Officer Turturro thinks the same. All right. In addition, Dr. Pittaluga has provided us with a further piece of information. He says that computer's practically useless."

There was another moment of silence. Well, a laptop that doesn't work is useless. Unless you want to hit somebody over the head with it, of course.

"Practically speaking," Fusco went on, "Pittaluga says the programs to make it work had not been installed. There was no program for using the Internet, and no way of viewing images or reading PDFs. Apart from a very simple text editor, there was nothing at all."

"I see." So to speak. "I'm sorry, but what about the files that—"

"They've been looked at by one of the conference delegates. Dr. Kawaguchi, to be precise. The man who helped us with the interviews."

"I see. So their contents—"

"Right now, their contents are of concern only to the investigating authorities. I'm sorry, Signor Viviani, but I wouldn't want to disturb your privacy with anything as trifling as a murder. In case we need you, don't worry, we'll call you. So go back to your croissants and have a nice day."

Needless to say, by the time he went back into the bar, these reprimands from the authorities—deserved as they were—had pissed him off all the more. In addition, he felt slightly disorientated. After the first moment of confusion, he had realized that Tiziana had asked him the previous day if she could tidy up the bar a little, but couldn't remember exactly what she'd intended to do. Above all, he hadn't thought she'd do it so quickly. All right, it's done now. Let's see if I like it. It's certainly brighter, I'll say that for her. The orange wall is really nice. The pictures aren't bad either. Abstract, of course. Anything too classical would be out of place, whereas abstract is always trendy, as those idlers who live off other people by claiming to be interior decorators would say. The Venetian blinds, though, have to go. Why are women so obsessed with curtains and blinds? It may be a stereotype but you can't deny there's a basis in truth. They love curtains and blinds, and hate—

And here Massimo, thinking of the world "soccer," realized that among the many things she'd added, installed, and painted in the room, Tiziana had also found time to take something away. At that very moment, the girl herself came into the bar, laden with bags.

"Hi. Can you give me a hand? I'm collapsing here."

"Right away," Massimo said, taking the bags. "I can well believe you're collapsing. With all the work you've been doing."

"Do you like it?"

"I will like it."

"You will like it?"

"I'll like it as soon as you bring back the poster of the Torino team and the front page of the *Gazzetta dello Sport*. As long as you haven't thrown them away. In which case, you'll have to buy them again."

"Listen, Massimo," Tiziana began, putting her hands out with the palms facedown, as if to say don't start breaking my balls, I've been working my guts out to make everything nice and all you can do is criticize. I tried to keep them. I really did. The fact is that with all the walls done, and the abstract paintings and everything looking so great, those two things really clashed. I couldn't find a place for them. Look," she added treacherously, "if you can see a place where they'd fit, then go ahead and put them back. They're there in the bin, I mean, in the drawer."

"Tiziana, I haven't a clue where they'd fit," Massimo said, emptying the contents of the bags into the pantry behind the counter. "I liked them where they were before."

Or rather, that's where they've always been.

"Because you're a lout with no taste."

What now? Quite apart from the accusation itself, that wasn't Tiziana's voice. Sure enough, rising to his full height again, Massimo saw Aldo standing in the middle of the bar, looking at the wall with obvious approval.

"Congratulations, Tiziana. You made me spend an afternoon at home watching television, but I have to say it was worth it. It's really great."

"Yes, it is," Rimediotti said, appearing in the doorway of the bar. "And it's so full of light, it really makes the place cheerful."

Two of them. I've only been open for three minutes and two of them are already here. Where were they, keeping watch out on the terrace?

"It is cheerful, isn't it?" Tiziana said. "I'm so relieved that you like it. Where are the others?"

"Oh, they'll be here soon . . . " Rimediotti said, still looking at the wall.

No sooner said than done. Simultaneously, or rather, almost simultaneously because otherwise they would have gotten stuck in the doorway, Ampelio and Del Tacca came in and looked around without saying anything.

"Well?" Tiziana said with a smile. "Do you like it?"

Still without saying anything, Ampelio went up to one of the two abstract paintings—a white background interrupted by a black line that twisted on itself to form two knots, which the artist had felt the need to fill with yellow and deep red, plus other scattered patches of color—and, craning his neck, started examining it.

"What's this?"

"It's a painting, Ampelio," Tiziana said with a smile. "By Mirò. *Man Facing Sun.*"

"Well, you can see he's been too long in the sun, poor man," Ampelio replied without taking his eyes off the painting. "He could at least have put a hat on. It must have gone to his head. Look what a mess he's made."

"I'd have thought it strange if you'd actually liked something," Tiziana said, still smiling.

"Why, do you like it?"

"Yes, I do. Otherwise I wouldn't have put it there, would I? Aldo, you have a bit of artistic sense, you tell him."

"Oh, please," Aldo replied, leaning on the counter. "Teaching Ampelio something about art is beyond my skills. Even though we've been to lots of museums."

"Oh, yes," Ampelio said with a laugh. "Back in the good old days."

"Museums? You two?"

"No, no, all four of us," Del Tacca said. "All four of us, and our wives too. It was on those package tours, where they put you on a bus at four in the morning and make you do nearly two hundred miles all in one go to get to where you're supposed to be. And don't even think about stopping to go to the toilet, because then you'll be late. Fortunately they sold pots on the bus, so if you couldn't hold out you'd take a pot and there you were. My God, when I think about it! But my wife wouldn't have missed one of those tours for the world, and the other wives were the same. We just had to tag along."

"I can imagine," Tiziana said. "So why was Ampelio laughing just now?"

"Because," Ampelio said, "as long as you were there, you had to find some way to have fun."

"I don't want to know," Tiziana said in a tone of voice that suggested exactly the opposite.

"It's a bit difficult to explain," Del Tacca said. "Aldo, do you still have the cassettes?"

"Of course I have them. I still listen to them from time to time."

"Bring them in tomorrow. It'll make it easier to tell the story. You'll have to be patient, Tiziana, we could tell you all about it now, but without the cassettes it'd be pointless. Anyway, we used to go to museums, and now if we're not careful they'll put us in a museum. Because old people are no use to anyone anymore and just break everyone's balls. Talking of old people, do we know anything about that Japanese professor?"

"Still dead," Ampelio said, continuing to wander about the bar.

"I wasn't talking to you, idiot," Del Tacca retorted. "I was talking to Massimo."

"What do you mean, know anything?"

"Massimo, don't you start being a dickhead too, please. Weren't you supposed to be going to the University this morning to look inside the computer?"

What? How can this old geezer possibly know everything that happens?

"How do you know that?"

"It was in the newspaper."

"Pilade, don't take the piss. Who told you?"

"No, no, I'm not taking the piss. Gino, tell Doubting Thomas here."

Rimediotti took a newspaper, obviously already read and reread, from the back pocket of his pants, unfolded it, and began in his clear expressionless voice: "'The mystery in the computer,' question mark. 'Pisa. A few hours after the unexpected death of Professor Kiminobu Asahara in unusual circumstances following a sudden illness, the investigators are now convinced that the death was not accidental. It has been ascertained beyond a doubt that in the hours immediately preceding his demise, the dead man had taken a large quantity of Tavor, and this drug appears to have been responsible for what proved to be a fatal respiratory arrest. But although the cause of death has been established, nothing else has emerged thus far from the investigation. The one clue available to the investigators seems to be the victim's laptop computer, to which he himself made reference in the days before his death, implying that its contents could cause trouble to one of his colleagues. In the light of these facts, the professor's laptop computer therefore assumes a key role in the case. In view of which, the investigators have arranged for a careful analysis of the contents of the said computer this morning, in collaboration with experts from the University, the outcome of which could be crucial to the investigation. It is in fact believed—'"

"All right, Gino, we get the drift," Del Tacca cut in.

"I can finish if you like."

"No, no, it doesn't matter." Del Tacca looked at Massimo. "You see? It was in the paper."

"I see. I have to say it's scary that not even the police can keep a secret in this town. It must be something in the air. But there's nothing in that article about me."

"Massimo, we weren't born yesterday," Aldo said.

"I know. I can see that."

"Are you calling me old? Elegant, you mean. Anyway, if I am old, you should give me a little respect and listen. Yesterday you were at the police station. This morning the laptop was taken to the University, to be shown to someone who would know what to do with it. Now, of all those who were at the police station yesterday, who was the only one who knows both the University and computers well enough to immediately find the right person for the job? Fusco?"

These old-timers. I underestimate them sometimes.

"Okay, okay, you got me. This morning I went to the University with Turturro, one of the officers from the station. We opened the computer, and the only thing interesting in it was two word documents. They seemed like notes. I say seemed because they were in Japanese. Fusco phoned me earlier to ask me if there was anything else in the computer."

"And what was in those notes?"

"Who knows? Fusco wouldn't say. But the fact that he asked me if there was anything else in the computer means there was nothing crucial."

"Not necessarily," Aldo said. "If he wouldn't tell you what was in the notes, then maybe it was something important."

"You're also right. But the fact remains, I don't know what was in those notes. And neither do any of you. So I think tonight you should talk about soccer, because there's nothing new on the murder."

"Hold on, Massimo," Del Tacca said. "If the notes were in Japanese, how did Fusco know what was in them?"

"He had a Japanese read them. Someone from the conference, who was also at the interviews yesterday as another interpreter. In fact, if you turn around you can see him. He just sat down at the table under the elm."

A huge mistake. Tiziana and the old-timers turned to look

at the table, where a young Japanese in a T-shirt and very narrow glasses had just sat down, after opening his own laptop with great care.

Now, every person interacts with other human beings according to the role he attributes to each of them. Faced with a teacher, there are those who listen and those whose minds wander, and at the sight of the Pope there are those who bow and those who get pissed off. In the same way, the presence of Kawaguchi caused somewhat different reactions inside the bar. Having classified the young man under the heading "customer," Tiziana took the menu and a notebook and came out from behind the counter. The old-timers, on the other hand, had immediately put the Japanese under the heading "our correspondent from the scene of the crime," and sat staring at him hungrily. The first to stir himself was Ampelio, who turned and said to Massimo, "Let's ask him!"

"All right," Massimo said. "You go."

"But I don't know a word of Japanese."

"That's no problem. He speaks English. All scientists speak English."

"Massimo," Aldo said, "you know Ampelio doesn't even speak Italian properly. You're the only one here who speaks English."

"That's what I thought. So in your opinion, what should I do?"

"Just go outside and ask him," Ampelio said in the tone of someone thinking, God, you're hard work.

"Then I haven't made myself clear. He's a customer who's just sat down to have a drink. I can't just go and ask him what was written in Asahara's notes. Maybe he wants to be left alone. Maybe he's the murderer, and feeling cornered will take out a samurai sword and cut me in half. Anyway I can't go and piss the customers off. That's out of the question."

"So what should we do?"

"How should I know? It isn't my problem. Send Rimediotti. Maybe he could show him a portrait of Mussolini and remind him we used to be allies. Maybe he'll be moved by that and you'll have managed to make contact."

"What's it got to do with me?" Rimediotti asked. "I don't even like the Japanese."

"I don't like them very much either," Del Tacca said. "I always find them distant."

"Of course," Aldo said. "They're hard-working people. I wish I had only Japanese customers at the restaurant. They like eating, they're very polite, they take photographs of the dishes, and in general they give you a satisfaction you don't find elsewhere. Unfortunately, I don't speak Japanese. Come on, Massimo, don't make us beg, just go. For once, don't be such a shirker."

"Nice try. Always resort to compliments in order to persuade people. There's no way I'm going."

The old-timers looked at each other as if the ground had been pulled from under their feet. The air filled with an embarrassed silence. Massimo walked to the coffee machine, and asked everyone, "I'm making myself a coffee. Does anyone want one?"

"Not me," Ampelio said in a reproving tone. "I already have a bitter taste in my mouth."

"I'd love a coffee," another voice said, as Massimo was turning to the machine to fill the filter. A not exactly unknown voice. And in fact, turning around, he saw the by now familiar face of Anton Snijders. The Dutchman hoisted himself onto a stool.

"How would you like it?"

"Macchiato, please."

"Macchiato, at this time of day?"

"Yes, why not?" Snijders asked in a sincere tone. "Don't you have any more milk?"

It was no use, he couldn't win. Massimo turned back to the machine. And as he inserted the filter holder, he heard Aldo's voice addressing Snijders in an unexpectedly polite tone:

"Professor, excuse me . . . "

"Go on."

"Could I ask you a favor?"

"Yes, of course."

"Oh, good. You speak English, don't you?"

Outside, at the table under the elm, Koichi Kawaguchi was puzzled. Ever since he had arrived in Pineta he had noticed this nice-looking café with the tables outside under the trees, and had seen that the café also had wi-fi, which was why, at the first opportunity, he had brought his laptop here, intending to read his mail in the shade while having a drink in peace and quiet. But, once he had looked inside the bar, the peace and quiet had hidden and was now refusing to come out. Basically, Koichi was starting to wonder how come, everywhere he went, that tall fellow with a face like a Taliban was also there. A waiter at the conference, an interpreter at the police station, and now a barman at the café. It wasn't possible. In addition, Koichi had the distinct feeling that they were talking about him inside the bar, and he could have sworn that once or twice one of the old men in there had even pointed at him with his thumb.

Maybe I'm imagining all this, he thought. But he wasn't convinced.

"I've got it," Snijders said, after the old-timers had summed up the situation for him, while Massimo pretended to be the diligent barman who despises all this idle chatter. "The one person who knows what was written in the files is that young man out there."

"Precisely," Aldo said, having apparently discovered hidden qualities in Snijders that he hadn't noticed before and now being quite courteous.

"Well, there's no harm in asking, I suppose. What is it you say In Italy? Asking is allowed . . . "

"And answering is polite," Rimediotti said.

"That's right. Well, I'll finish my coffee and then I'll go."

"Excuse me, Professor," Ampelio said, "could I ask you something else?"

"Go on."

"While you're about it, could you also ask the guy if he'd be so kind as to move to another table?"

EIGHT

A few minutes had passed. Inside the bar, Massimo was getting everything ready for the evening aperitif. It was the end of May, and as was the case every year, the arrival of good weather caused whole gangs of idlers and layabouts, their ages ranging from the proud twenties to the grudgingly accepted forties, to emerge from their lethargy and enjoy a glass of something accompanied by free appetizers as the first stage in those fine summer evenings (aperitif-dinner-discotheque) that punctuated their pointless lives.

Massimo had always attached a great deal of importance to this custom. Firstly, the more people came, the better it was, both in terms of income and in terms of popularity. Secondly, once the trays of appetizers had been prepared, you just had to pour the drinks and make sure that people paid, and for the barman, all things considered, it was a chaotic but pleasant hour. Especially if the barman was a divorced thirty-seven-year-old who, outside the bar, had the social life of a clam. In addition, the old-timers were usually at home at this hour, and Massimo's mood could not help but improve. Usually.

This evening, however, the old-timers were still there, at the table under the elm, absentmindedly playing canasta while waiting for Snijders to extort some fresh daily news from Kawaguchi. Snijders had indeed sauntered over to Kawaguchi's table, had started talking, and had somehow got him to move to a round table near the tamarisks, and now the two were chatting away like old friends. After a while, out of

THREE-CARD MONTE · 125

the corner of his eye, Massimo saw Kawaguchi stand up, shake Snijders' hand, and leave.

Look, I may be becoming an old gossip, but who gives a damn. I'm the one who had the idea and took that computer to Carlo, I deserve a modicum of satisfaction. Massimo looked at the trays, judged them to be perfectly arranged, turned, and asked Tiziana in the most natural tone possible, "Tiziana, we still need the tabouleh and the tuna bites. Can you see to them? I'm going outside for a moment."

"Yes, bwana, Tiziana see to everything. Bwana not to worry, just go outside for nice gossip."

Massimo took a cigarette, went out, and went straight to the table under the elm, where Snijders had just joined the sprightly crew. He took a chair, sat down, and was greeted by Ampelio with a malevolent, "I thought you had work to do."

"Come on, Grandpa, don't break my balls," Massimo replied, lighting his cigarette. "If the professor knows something, I don't see what's so bad about hearing it. Seeing that he's telling you guys, in about thirty seconds the whole town will know about it anyway."

"He did say something," Snijders said. "Oh, and please, my name is Anton. Professor's too pompous. That young man and I had a nice conversation. About science to start with, just to be friendly. He's doing some good work, as it happens. A bit strange, but very interesting."

To you, the old men's eyes said. Not to us. Just come to the point, we have to go home for dinner and we don't know anything yet.

"Then we talked a little about the conference, and finally I asked him about the computer. Just like that, indirectly. He told me there was nothing in the files on the computer but haiku."

Silence. Then, after two or three seconds, Aldo started laughing.

"Do you mind telling us the joke?" Pilade said. "Maybe we can have a laugh too."

"I'm sorry. But I think the guy's pulling our legs. Haiku are poems."

"Poems?" Ampelio asked.

Snijders nodded with a smile.

"Poems," Aldo went on. "They're typically Japanese. I don't know much about it, but I seem to remember they're very short, just three lines, inspired by a seasonal theme like summer, spring—"

"Yes, autumn and then winter," Del Tacca cut in. "So now we have all the seasons. But wasn't that Japanese guy just pulling your leg?"

"I know what you mean," Snijders said. "But I really don't think he was. He also said that he seemed to remember that Asahara wrote poetry. It was a hobby of his."

"O.K. So what of it?"

"Well, if the only thing on the computer was poems, then I don't know what's so important about that computer."

"But I know," Massimo said.

"Oh, so you know, do you?" Ampelio said.

"More than you, anyway. When we questioned the Japanese, one of Asahara's colleagues said that he'd never seen that computer before, and that Asahara usually used a different one. The others confirmed that, but nobody was able to say if Asahara had brought two computers with him or only one."

"What system did the computer use?" Snijders asked. "Do you know?"

"Yes. Of course. I saw the system folders. It was definitely Linux. What version, I don't know."

"No, I wasn't thinking of the version. I was thinking that I heard Asahara's seminar. It was very clearly done with PowerPoint."

"Ah. I understand."

"Congratulations," Del Tacca said. "But we don't understand a damn thing. Can someone explain?"

"It's not complicated," Massimo said. "In order to function, a computer needs what's called an operating system, which is simply a collection of more or less complex commands that act as an interpreter between the user's intentions and the computer itself. Usually, a computer has only one operating system, although in theory it's possible to have more than one on the same machine. There are basically three operating systems around at the moment: Windows, Linux, and Macintosh. All clear so far?"

We're not that stupid, said Aldo's eyebrows.

"Now, Anton says that Asahara's seminar used PowerPoint, which is a kind of editor that can be used on Windows and, with a few modifications, on Mac, but not on Linux. Linux has a very similar editor, which is called OpenOffice, but visually the two are easy to tell apart. That's why, if Asahara's seminar used PowerPoint, that means only one thing. That it had been prepared on another computer."

"Ah," Del Tacca said. "But can't you move these things between computers of two different kinds?"

"In theory, yes, there's a certain amount of compatibility, but for graphic presentations I don't think that anybody of sound mind would even consider it. He'd be wasting a whole lot of time."

What's all this about sound mind? First I said it to Fusco, and now to Pilade. As if everyone who was sane had to behave like me.

"I see. So what you mean is that this guy had two computers with him."

"That's possible. Or else he prepared the seminar somewhere else, and brought it with him on a memory stick or something like that. Which seems the most likely thing to me.

I don't see why anybody needs to go around with two computers."

"Lucky you," Ampelio said. "I don't even understand why you have to go around with one. You're in Italy, you're from another part of the world, and instead of having a look around, you bring your computer with you. Everybody takes their computer with them nowadays. First everyone took their cell phone with them, now everyone takes their computer. If we carry on like this, in three or four years we'll have to go around with a wheelbarrow. Do me a favor."

"Grandpa, this is a bit different. These people work with computers."

"Good for them. When they're at a conference they work, and when the conference takes a break they rush to their computers and carry on working. A good thing you people are there, what can I say? I remember my poor dad."

"I'm sorry, but why?" Massimo asked, trying to imagine his great-grandfather Remo, whom he had never known, with his spade over his shoulder, stooped over a computer and surfing the Internet after a hard day in the fields.

"Because my dad always said that when they're dying nobody ever complains that they didn't work enough."

It was 8:30, and the flood had receded, leaving only a few stragglers who sat around waiting to decide how to continue the evening. The old-timers had gone home to put their feet under their respective tables for a well-deserved dinner, Tiziana was going back and forth, bringing in the glasses and everything else from outside, and the only people still inside were Massimo and Snijders, the latter having spent the preceding hour sitting on the stool, chatting with a few conference delegates who had ended up in the bar.

Once they were alone, as if they had come to an agreement, they had started talking about the Asahara case, and had found themselves in agreement on the need to somehow find out if Asahara really had had two computers with him.

"There's one thing we can do," Snijders said. "We can phone the secretary of the conference, Signora Ricciardi, and ask if she remembers if Asahara had his own computer or not."

"Hmmm. Maybe. Do you think she'd remember?"

"I don't know. But let me explain. Usually there's an official computer at the conference, but if someone wants to work with his own he connects it instead of the official one and uses that. So Asahara may either have given the organizers the slides of his conference on a memory stick, or used his own computer. Someone in the organization should know. I tried to ask my colleagues who were here before, I even told them why I was asking, but nobody can remember."

There you go. Discretion above all, even for you. It's no use, I get all the gossips.

"I see. Well, we could try. If you like, I have Signora Ricciardi's cell phone number. You can call straight away if you want."

"Isn't it better if you call her?"

"No, trust me. I quarreled with that woman by phone every day for a week. I don't feel up to calling, and if she heard my voice she'd probably hang up immediately."

"All right. If you can give me the number . . . "

"Here it is, on this piece of paper."

"O.K., where's the phone?"

"There, behind the ice cream counter."

As Snijders went to the phone, Massimo started to let his mind wander. It struck him as strange that someone should have two computers with him. Grandpa was right, even one's too many. Careful, Massimo. Never judge what other people might do on the basis of what you would do. For example, I'd never have cheated on my wife. Not that I ever had any opportunities. I never had them before, and I don't think the situation's going to improve as I get older. No, let's think about the murder, that's better. At least for once something bad happened to someone else. Maybe Asahara was someone who liked to think ahead. And, given that a laptop was stolen on the very first day of the conference, he wasn't completely wrong. I'm not convinced, though. I don't know, let's hear what the Ricciardi woman said. If she remembers anything. But it'll be difficult.

Instead of which, Snijders came back smiling from ear to ear. When he got to the counter, he sat down on the stool and started to nod.

"I was right. Signora Ricciardi remembers that Asahara came to the conference with his own computer. She says she remembers it well, because she had to look for an adaptor."

"Of course, to adapt the plug on his machine to our sockets. The plugs vary from country to country."

"Yes, God knows why. Anyway, there we are. Asahara had another computer. A computer that used Windows. I'm not a betting man, but I reckon there's a good chance I'd win if I bet that that's the computer we have to look at." Snijders continued, nodding. "And I'm not the only one."

"How do you mean?"

"Signora Ricciardi told me the police are in the hotel, searching all the rooms. I say they're looking for that computer."

"Quite likely," Massimo said. "Which means we're fucked."

"I wouldn't go that far."

"Sorry, I spend so much time with these seventy-year-olds, I'm starting to talk like them. I meant that if there was another computer, God knows what's happened to it by now. Even supposing the motive for the murder is connected to what Asahara said, if the culprit wanted to steal or destroy one of the files, whether or not he wanted to copy it, the first thing he'd have done, if he was clever, is throw the computer in the sea.

Three days have gone by, he had plenty of time to do it. And I don't think there are that many stupid people at a chemistry conference."

"I wouldn't necessarily say that. But you're right. So . . . "

"So we go back to doing what we do best. You can be a scientist, I can be a barman. Because without that computer, the one possible shred of evidence goes up in smoke, and we don't have anything to go on."

Snijders sat there on the stool, visibly disappointed. He made a little grimace, then got off the stool.

"Are you going to dinner?" Massimo asked. He was starting to feel the need to be alone for a while, given that he had a few things to do. Since the bar is supposed to be mine, and since Tiziana is stopping every few seconds to admire the wall, clearly pleased with her handiwork, which means I can't really count on her help, guess who's going to be the only one to do any work tonight? Unfortunately, it seemed that Snijders did not have the slightest intention of leaving.

"No, when I'm alone I eat as it comes." He glanced beyond the counter, at the cured meats on display in the back room. "Maybe a sandwich . . . Could I have a sandwich?"

"Of course. I'll make you one right now. Venison ham, spinach, and walnut oil."

"Do you have anything else?"

"Spinach, walnut oil, and venison ham. There are four other possibilities, but I'll spare you those. Trust me, it's very good."

"All right."

"Would you like something to drink with it?" Massimo asked, hoping the man wouldn't want milk with his meal: something the Dutch, as he had learned in several years as a barman, were quite capable of.

"A beer, please."

Thank God for that. Massimo went into the back room, put

the ham into the slicer, and started to slice. As he was making the sandwich, Snijders went on, "is it far from here to San Gimignano?"

"It's quite a way. At least two hours by car."

"Oh, yes, that is far."

"You could get there and back in a day without any problem. Although there are plenty of things to see around here, without having to go all the way to San Gimignano."

"Yes, I'm sure there are," Snijders replied, in a tone that suggested he was thinking: But I wanted to go to San Gimignano. "It's just that, without the conference, there isn't much to do here. And even the conference wasn't very . . . " Snijders made a strange noise with his mouth.

"Wasn't it interesting? Maybe it was a bit off-topic for you."

"Yes, that too, but not just that. These days I always seem to hear the same things. It's rare to find a bit of imagination, of inventiveness. The Italians in particular are strange. When it comes to expertise, I mean."

Yes, we're very strange, my friend, when it comes to expertise. You're in a country where models talk about soccer and priests talk about sex and families.

"In what way?"

"They aren't original. Almost never, I mean. Lately I've seen people who are doing the same things they were doing twenty years ago. They refine the work, they perfect it. They do wonderful things sometimes. Very complex things. But always using the same models. I mean, I'm generalizing. There are exceptions. But they're rare. And that's not what science is. You need originality, new ideas. It's industry that has to apply them. We have to do the research."

Breaking news. New hot water spring discovered in the locality of Pineta by Professor Snijders from the University of Groningen.

"And I don't understand the reason," Snijders went on,

clearly passionate about the subject. "Scientifically speaking, the Italians have always been strong. Well taught as students. Not like the Russians, or the Indians, but much better than the European average. It's strange."

Massimo felt cut to the quick. The subject had made his blood boil so many times, even involuntarily, that hearing it talked about set off a Pavlovian reflex in him.

"It is strange," he said as he handed Snijders the sandwich on a plate. "You know why? Research in Italy isn't original because it's commissioned by dinosaurs. In Italy, forty-seven percent of full professors are over sixty. Sixty. Gioacchino Rossini couldn't be original at sixty, and you want people like that to succeed?"

"But why don't they retire?" Snijders asked with his mouth full. "Don't they realize that they're not doing any good?"

"No. They don't realize. Because in this damned country we're used to doing good in a morbid way. I'll give you a simple example. A lot of the professors say, 'I can't retire now, even though I'm entitled to and even though I don't want to do a damn thing anymore, because first I have to sort out my graduate student, my research fellow, or whatever I call my current slave.' The concept is that since this person has done his thesis, his doctorate, and everything else with me as his supervisor, I have a kind of moral obligation to sort him out. Of course. The pity of it is that if only you packed your bags and left, you'd release enough money for three, and I mean three, researchers. But maybe then your protégé wouldn't qualify. Especially if he's a complete dickhead whose only gift is stubbornness. Because the fact is that in the last few years people haven't gotten into university in Italy because they're good. They've gotten in because they have nowhere else to go. And that's the first problem."

"Oh, you mean there's a second problem?" Snijders asked, chewing on his sandwich.

"Oh, yes. The second problem is that there are too many young people. And too many of them are totally unsuited. I saw people who as undergraduates had difficulty passing exams being accepted as graduate students. And why was that? Because those candidates who were better than them had enough initiative to go abroad, or to go to work outside the university. Whereas those who couldn't even wipe their own asses stayed, and started the whole rigmarole. The contract, the doctorate, the scholarship, the research fellowship, and all the rest of that crap. Let's be clear, the professors have their fair share of blame in all this. Instead of setting a ceiling to guarantee quality, they've continued to take a fixed number of people, a number that's too large in relation to what they'd be able to absorb in the future. So, along with good people who deserved to do their doctorate and stay to do research, they've collected the dead and the wounded. People who, after starting at the age of twenty-five, are twenty-eight by the time they've finished their doctorate, and thirty or thirty-two after the research fellowship. And at that point, unless they're hired as guinea pigs by the pharmaceutical industry, they're stuck, because right now industry doesn't want a thirty-two-year-old graduate, not even one with a doctorate, and not even if he comes free and gift-wrapped. I should know. I'm one of them."

"How do you mean?" Snijders asked, having in the meantime finished his sandwich, scarily, in about thirty seconds flat.

Massimo puffed briefly through his nose and smiled. If only you knew. "It's rather a long story," he said.

"Take as long as you like," Snijders replied. "I need time to digest."

I can believe that. Well, if that's the way it is . . .

Massimo was quite reluctant to tell the story of how he had moved from a computer monitor to a bar counter. Firstly, because he didn't believe that people could possibly be all that interested in what concerned him. Secondly, because he didn't really think it put him in a good light.

"I graduated in mathematics in exactly four years. In November of the fourth year. And I started on my doctorate in January of the following year. I don't how interested you are in the subject I was supposed to be studying, but anyway, it was to do with the mathematics of string theory."

Snijders raised his eyebrows. "I don't know anything about that."

"Don't worry, you're in good company. I don't say that as a joke. The subject I was supposed to be dealing with was extremely complicated, and when I started my postgraduate studies I felt as if I'd wandered into a nightmare. The more I studied, the less I understood. Sometimes, I had the feeling I'd grasped something, then immediately afterwards, I found another article that demolished that idea. The worst thing in all this was that I had the impression that even my thesis supervisor, who as it happens was a physicist, didn't understand a damn thing about what I was doing. Let's be clear about this, I don't blame him: he was quite an elderly man, and this particular subject was quite new and really complicated. But, after a while, the suspicion started to weigh on me. Then, one day, I went to him with a pile of articles and a page of questions. To cut a long story short, that was when I realized he didn't understand anything about the subject either. Worse, the doubts I'd been having hadn't even occurred to him. I was much further ahead than the person who should have been guiding me, and at the same time, I was completely in the dark. When I left his office, I looked at myself in the mirror. You know what the most important gift is for a mathematician?"

"I have no idea. Intelligence, maybe."

"No. It's important, but not by itself. No, the fundamental gift a mathematician needs is humility. The humility to admit when you haven't understood something, and not try to fool yourself that you have. If you haven't understood something, or you aren't convinced, don't take it as read. If you do that, you'll only get hurt. You must be absolutely honest with yourself. Well, as far as mathematics was concerned I always tried to be honest with myself. And the only conclusion I could possibly reach was that I wasn't good enough. I wasn't cut out for that kind of work, it was beyond my capabilities. If I'd continued, I'd have been wasting time and deceiving myself."

Snijders looked at him. With one finger, he pointed at the bar. "So . . . "

"Precisely. You see, I'm a fussy kind of person. Things have to be done the way I say, and if they aren't, well, I tend to get upset. I'm pleased with myself when I do something well, and it doesn't really matter what it is. Anyway, just before these things happened, I'd come into a bit of money. Not a fortune, but enough to open a bar. And I realized that I preferred life to a career. I chose to be an excellent barman, rather than a frustrated mathematician."

"And doesn't it bother you? Don't you think someone like you is wasted in a bar?"

"It depends. Sometimes, if I think about the time I spent poring over my books, I could hit myself. But, if I am the person I am, I also owe it to everything that I studied. If 'owe' is the right word. But do I feel wasted? No, absolutely not. I'm much more useful to the world, doing a job I like, than one of those sons of bitches who ends up in an executive position, creates an unexplained deficit the size of the Grand Canyon, and then gives himself a massive golden handshake when he's forced to resign. And besides, working in a bar isn't so bad."

Snijders looked at him. He didn't seem terribly convinced. "Really? Isn't it a bit boring?"

"Yes," Massimo said, as he walked to the back room. "Sometimes it is. But I don't mind that. And besides, sometimes a boring job can bring out the best in a person."

Snijders smiled. "Now you're pulling my leg."

Not completely, Massimo thought. A boring job can bring out the best in a person. Don't think about what you're doing, go onto automatic pilot, and let your brain keep ticking over. When he developed the theory of relativity, Einstein was working in a patent office. Böll was a census gatherer, and Bulgakov a country doctor. Pessoa worked for the land registry office, I think. Borges was a librarian, and Cavafy an employee of the water company.

Give an imaginative man a dull, repetitive job, one that puts him in contact with other people, and there's a strong possibility you'll produce a Nobel Prize winner. Often, left to his own devices, someone who isn't constantly plagued by the anxiety of having to produce lets his thoughts settle of their own free will, so that they gradually sink to the bottom and crystallize, sometimes, into forms of rare beauty. Of course, I spend my free afternoons slumped on the couch playing computer games, but that's another matter. I'm not a poet.

Fortunately, while Massimo's thoughts were in danger of moving in a depressing direction, Del Tacca came in, followed by Ampelio.

"Good evening," Pilade said, while Ampelio went and sat down at a table. "What are you two talking about?"

"About the fact that Massimo is a perfect barman," Snijders said, pointing emphatically at Massimo.

"Who, him?" Ampelio said. "For heaven's sake. And you listen to him?"

"I'm not perfect," Massimo admitted. "But I am way above average. What, the hell, I only use fresh produce. I have six different types of coffee. I have almost forty types of beer. This is the only bar within a radius of twelve miles that does granita with freshly squeezed fruit juice, and not with synthetic syrups. And now I have an orange wall, so I'm up-to-date on an aesthetic level too. I'd even have wi-fi, if a flock of elderly pains in the butt hadn't made their nest on the one table where it works. Be that as it may, the fact remains that I'm the barman, that this is my bar, and that from today onwards, conversations about murders, deaths, and premeditated tragedies are banned. Now, can I get you anything?"

NINE

S o. Now I have to go to the Internet café to get a signal. Then I have to phone the Ricciardi woman to find out when they're planning to pay me, because even though the conference has been suspended I still did two days. Aldo should have done it, but there you are. He's an artist in his soul and doesn't think about money. Then I have to find a way to get that Venetian blind off the door of the bar. Is there anything else? Let's see. Oh, yes, I have to go to the municipal police to get the permit for the tables. And then? It seems to me there's something else, but I can't remember what. You know what, who cares? It'll probably come back to me. An hour after I was supposed to have done it, as usual.

Walking to the Internet café, Massimo was repeating in his head the list of Things to Do Today, which constituted one of his usual nightmares.

The fact was, Massimo's memory was starting to work in a similar way to a pipe: events going back months or even years, whether important or not, furred up the walls of the pipe and were almost impossible to get rid of. Whereas information that Massimo acquired constantly in the course of the day, regardless of its importance, entered, ran through the pipe for a limited period, then came out the other end and was gone. At the same time, Massimo prided himself on having an excellent memory and so never wrote down what he was supposed to, which was why when he had a list of commitments to fulfill he went over them in his mind every thirty seconds, with results that didn't always live up to expectations.

On the other hand, Massimo was trying desperately not to think about the murder. And to do this, the only possible way was to find something to do to fill his brain and the day. Having discovered that Asahara's computer contained absolutely nothing, Massimo had been forced to look reality in the face. The hypothesis they had all started from was already very flimsy, and they had nothing else to back it up with. So that was the end of it. But since Massimo hated leaving something half done or not understanding something, in order not to feel really pissed off he needed to find something else to occupy him. Starting with the problem that had been tormenting him in the background for some days now, in other words: why doesn't the wi-fi work in my bar?

That was why Massimo was on his way to the ConnectZone, the only Internet café in Pineta, with the aim of asking the owner if he too had had these problems, and if he had, how he had solved them. Broadly speaking, our hero hated asking favors of people if he didn't know them very well, but the guy at the Internet café was an easygoing type, and Massimo liked him because whenever he came to the bar he'd take the newspapers, read them, and then put them back in their place perfectly folded, just as he had found them. Details, maybe, but Massimo couldn't understand people who took the newspaper, separated the pages, and then after reading it flung it back together as best they could or just left it there all screwed up, as if the newspaper were theirs and not the bar's.

Reaching the Internet café, Massimo went in and looked around. Four or five people were sitting at the computers, among whom Massimo recognized two or three conference delegates: an obese American professor, Asahara's Japanese colleague Dr. Kubo, and a German with a face like a hit man whom Massimo remembered well because, during the first coffee break, he had refilled his plate a dozen times. He went to the back room, where the owner's wife was reading a book while nibbling at strawberries from a small bag.

"Hello. I was looking for Davide."

"Hi. Davide isn't here."

"Ah. Do you know when he will be?"

"Oh, he won't be in this morning because he's at home waiting for the boiler man, our boiler broke down the other day and we've had only cold water for the past two days. Can I help in any way?"

"I don't know, maybe you can. It's about my wireless connection. I installed it a week ago, but I'm having a few problems. Basically I can only get a signal in one spot. I wanted to know if you had similar problems."

"I see. Listen, I don't really know. Davide set it all up, and we haven't had any problems like that. Mind you, we don't use the wireless connection much, people usually come and sit down at one of our desktops. But nobody's ever complained about there not being any signal."

I knew it. Sometimes I get the feeling certain things happen only to me.

"I see."

"Anyway, Davide will be here for lunch. I could ask him to go to your bar for a coffee after lunch, that way you can ask him yourself."

"Okay, let's do that. Thanks."

Thing to Do Number One, still outstanding. Oh, well, never mind. Now what do I have to do? Oh yes, phone the Ricciardi woman, and then go to the municipal police. Or rather, wait: as I'm already out, first I'll go to the police and then I'll phone the witch.

Massimo took a cigarette from the pack, looked at it, decided he'd smoke after going to the police, and put it back. Then he walked to the crossing and started to cross the avenue. Having reached the middle, he stopped and closed his eyes.

A cyclist with a mustache, who had taken it for granted that someone crossing the street wouldn't suddenly stop, missed him by half an inch and turned without stopping to say something blasphemous but, given the circumstances, well-deserved. Massimo stood still in the middle of the roadway, with his eyes closed.

After a few seconds, he heard the sound of a car horn interspersed with curses. He opened his eyes and saw that a column of seven or eight cars had formed by his side, their drivers understandably impatient to go where they had to go and with absolutely no desire to have barmen messing them around. Massimo ran to the sidewalk and carried on walking, trying not to take any notice of the insults being hurled in his direction. As he advanced, his breath came ever quicker and he felt his face tingle with emotion.

Calm down, calm down. It may just be a coincidence. You may have it all wrong. Now go to the bar and think about it for a moment. There must be something I can do. First of all, though, I have to understand what it means. It means something, I'm sure of that. I'd bet my balls on it. Not that they're any use to me these days anyway. Right, stop bullshitting and try to concentrate for a moment.

While Massimo was trying to concentrate, the telephone rang. He lifted the receiver mechanically, and thanks entirely to his parasympathetic nervous system managed to come out with a distracted "Hello."

"Oh, you're there, are you? I've been ready for half an hour."

"Grandpa?" Massimo said.

"You're a dickhead, you know that?" Ampelio continued. "You've been a dickhead for more than thirty years now. I've been waiting half an hour."

Oh, God. Today's the twenty-fifth. The post office. I forgot to take Grandpa to the post office. That's what it was.

On the twenty-fifth of every month, Ampelio went to the post office to withdraw his well-earned pension. Which, to tell the truth, he could have had paid directly into his own post office account. Unfortunately every attempt to persuade the old man to have his pension paid into his account was rejected by him on the basis of the following sequence of arguments:

1) The only money you have is what you spend, and if it's in my account I won't touch it.

2) I'm already eighty-three and could kick the bucket tomorrow morning, and when I'm in hell I can do whatever I like with my money.

3) You can all fuck off anyway.

Given the untouchability of the Ampelian *Weltanschauung*, then, on the twenty-fifth of every month the Great Architect created on this Earth, Ampelio had to be picked up and taken to withdraw his pension. Ever since he had gotten his license, this had fallen to Massimo, for the simple reason that his first car had been a gift from none other than Ampelio himself. The twenty-fifth of every month. Including today.

"Yes, Grandpa," Massimo said, trying to navigate the uncommon situation of having to be nice to his grandfather. "You'll have to be patient. I've had a bit of a tough morning, and I forgot."

"Oh, great! He forgot. Look, I'm the one who's eighty-something. You're fifty years younger than me. If there's any-one here who has a right to forget things, it's me, not you! The problem is, you only have a memory for the things that inter-est you. The bar, yes. Mathematics, yes. Soccer too. Your grandfather, no. Because you don't give a damn about your grandfather! The day I die you'll regret how you treated me. He forgot! Do me a favor . . . "

"Grandpa, why don't you do *me* a favor for once and get

someone else to take you to the post office. I'll explain later, okay? Bye."

And he slammed the phone down.

That's it! I've got it. All it took was someone saying the right word. I'm going to have to say thank you to my grandfather. Of course, I may be wrong. There's only one way to find out.

Massimo took a deep breath, then picked up the phone again. As he was dialing the number he realized he was out of breath, and tried taking two or three deep breaths to calm down. At the third ring, a female voice answered:

"Good morning, Department of Chemistry."

"Good morning." Deep breath. "I'd like to speak to Carlo Pittaluga."

"One moment."

After a brief wait, luckily not disturbed by inane music, he heard Carlo's voice:

"Yes, hello."

"Hi, Carlo." Extra deep breath. "Sorry to keep bothering you, but I need a favor. It's vital that you do it immediately. Do you still have the stuff that was in the Japanese professor's computer?"

"The files? One moment, I may have deleted them but I'm not sure. I'll have a look."

There was a brief silence, broken only by the frantic clicking of the mouse.

"Yes, it's all there. What do you want me to do? Shall I send it to you?"

"No. You should try running the program."

"What?"

"In one of the two folders there was a program in Fortran. A program for molecular dynamics. Do you remember?"

"Yes, yes. Here it is. A simple little program. Probably for educational purposes."

"Good. Please, can you try to compile it and run it?"

"Well . . . why not?" Carlo laughed. "What's supposed to happen? Will it give us the name of the murderer?"

"It's possible. In a way. I'll explain later. Will you call me when you've done it?"

"All right. But I don't know how long it's going to take to run it."

"It doesn't matter. Try to compile it, anyway."

"Right away, sir. See you later."

Massimo put the phone down. He picked up the pack of cigarettes and took one out. Now I really need one. He lit it, took a few drags, and tried to relax. Pointless. He was in such an emotional state that he was shaking. He took another few drags, then stubbed out the cigarette in the ashtray. At that moment the telephone rang.

Massimo picked up the receiver and said, "Hello."

"I see you're still there." It was Ampelio. "Who brought you up, King Kong? When I was young, if I'd slammed the phone down like that, you know what would have happened?"

"Grandpa, when you were young they still used smoke signals. I need to keep the phone clear. I'll pick you up in five minutes, okay? Bye."

And he hung up. After a moment, the phone rang again. This time Massimo picked up cautiously.

"Hello."

"Hello, Massimo." It was Carlo's voice. "Listen, I tried to compile the program, but there's a problem."

"What problem?" Massimo asked.

"It doesn't work. It's too big. In fact, it's ridiculously big. Theoretically, this program will require more than forty gigabytes."

Massimo moved the receiver away from his ear, while the shaking in his legs receded and the tightness in his chest vanished as if someone had magicked it away. He was surprised not to hear a triumphal march.

I don't believe it. I actually got it.

After a few seconds, he heard Carlo's voice again: "What should I do, reduce the size and send it?"

"No, Carlo. It doesn't matter. It's perfect as it is."

"Oh. All right. Will you explain sometime?"

"Of course. At least I hope so. Listen, I'll call you later. Thanks."

After hanging up, Massimo was silent for about ten seconds. Of course, I'm still not one hundred percent sure. Actually, I'm not sure at all. It's a theory. But right now there's only one thing I can do.

Massimo picked up the receiver for the umpteenth time and dialed a number. At the second ring, a mild voice replied, "Pineta Police Station."

"Good morning. This is Massimo Viviani. I'd like to speak to Inspector Fusco."

"One moment, please."

H aving phoned the police station, and come to an agreement with Fusco about what to do, there remained half an hour to go pick up his grandfather and take him to get his paws on his long-awaited pension. A task which, as can be imagined, Massimo hated and feared at the same time.

Firstly, Ampelio liked to be taken to the post office early in the morning, by nine at the latest. There, he found a way of chatting with the people he knew (in other words, everybody) without somehow losing his place in the line, which he defended verbally and with distracted but intentional blows with his stick on the tibias of anyone trying to cut in front of him. After which, having pocketed the cash, he remained where he was, calmly talking to the cashier on duty, completely ignoring the counterpoint of comments—I'd happily kill people who do that, oh but the poor man's old, I'm old too though I was young when I came in here, there should be a trap door in front of the counter so that when someone wastes time the cashier just pulls a lever and hey presto—coming thick and fast behind his back. As a result, in terms of time, the operation required no less than an hour and a half, during which the bar was in the hands of Tiziana on overtime pay.

Secondly, the car ride was a genuine ordeal because Ampelio, although not himself at the wheel, always found a way to say something in his fine stentorian voice to any motorist whose driving did not satisfy his personal rules of correctness: the one who goes too fast ("Carry on, the trees seem solid enough"), the one who goes too slowly ("What are you carrying, eggs? Can you sell me a couple?"), the one who uses his horn too much ("Blow that thing when you go to see your mother, there's always a traffic jam there") and so on. Of course, if anyone took offense, it would be Massimo they got angry with, not that nice old man in the beret.

Having picked up Ampelio outside his building, Massimo had just set off in the direction of the post office when Ampelio said, "Listen, Massimo, Pilade and I have been thinking."

"I'm already shaking. Go on."

"What do you mean, shaking, you moron? It's in your own interest. Tell me, how would you feel if we left the table under the elm free?"

"I'd feel fine. Have you found another bar that'll let you in?"

"What are you talking about? We're staying there. We'll just move to another spot."

"And where would that be? The last time you all came inside you made me switch off the air-conditioning. And it was July, I don't know if you remember."

"Not outside and not inside. Behind."

"Behind?"

"Well behind. In the open space next to Toncelli's garden."

The open space to which Ampelio was referring was a strip of ground, about three yards wide, that ran alongside the wall to the west of the bar, and which you reached through a door at the back. Shady certainly, given that it was overlooked on one side by the hedge of old Toncelli's garden, but on the other long side it was completely hemmed in by the wall of the bar. Too narrow and too oppressive, in his judgment, to put tables there. But if they liked it . . .

"Well, if it's okay for you it's certainly okay for me. I'll take a table for four and put it next to the door."

"No, no, we don't need tables. They'll take up too much space."

"But what else do you need the space for?"

"For the bowling green, right? If you put a table there, it'll be too short. Without a table it's almost 25 yards, it's not quite regulation, but it'll certainly do."

"Do for whom? For you, maybe. Not for me."

Bowls, can you imagine? I already have the four of you on my back all day long, morning and night, you're part of the furniture by now. If I put in a bowling green as well, I'm done for. I'll have all the pensioners in Pineta waiting in line inside the bar. I don't have any desire to put denture adhesive next to the soap in the bathroom. I'll stick landmines under that space. Forget about bowls.

"Listen to him! Tiziana puts those things up on the walls and he doesn't say a word, but if I suggest something, no way. What difference will it make if you put in a bowling green? Will it frighten people away?"

"Grandpa, you're changing the kind of bar this is. If we sell peanuts, our customers will be monkeys. If we put in a bowling green, our customers will be veterans of the Africa campaign. It's the law of supply and demand. At the moment, I already have my daily dose of seniors to put up with. I have no intention of increasing it for the next thirty years."

Ampelio grunted. In the meantime, they had arrived at the post office.

"You're just being stupid, as far as I can see. All right, let me get out. Park the car, come inside, we'll talk it over, and you'll see I'm right."

Massimo parked, let his grandfather get out, watched him walk toward the post office, then as soon as Ampelio was at a safe distance, he started the car again and set off in the direction of the police station.

That's all I need right now, to talk about bowls.

*

Massimo was sitting in the now familiar armchair without casters, looking at Inspector Fusco. Who in his turn was looking at Massimo. This had been going on, in silence, for about thirty seconds.

A few minutes earlier, Massimo had arrived at the police station and had told Fusco what had occurred to him that morning and what he had asked Carlo to do. Then he had offered Fusco his explanation.

Now he was waiting.

After a few more seconds, Fusco got up out of his armchair with casters. "It's a mess," he said.

I know, Massimo thought.

"It's a mess for various reasons," Fusco continued, resting his buttocks on the windowsill. "Reason number one, because if you're wrong we create an unprecedented diplomatic incident. And I screw up my career. Reason number two, because now it's certain that the man was poisoned here, in Italy. So the case is ours without a shadow of a doubt. And beyond what you've just told me, I don't have a scrap of a clue."

Fusco looked at his fingers, then put his hands together and started to open and close his fingertips rhythmically. He didn't seem too convinced.

"Listen, I can't promise anything. We can try. Or rather, we have to try. But we need to tread very carefully. One wrong word and it could all blow up in our faces. The police interpreter has already gone back to Florence and I don't have time to call him back. That's why we have to do like the other time. But you have to realize that I can only start with general questions. To be able to ask more specific questions, I need something to grab onto, an inconsistency, something like that. You translate what I say, exactly, without adding a single word. Is that clear?"

"Of course."

"All right, then. And if it all blows up, amen." Fusco pressed the button on the intercom. "Galan? We need to summon a couple of people. Would you please go to the Santa Bona and kindly, and I mean kindly, ask Dr. Shin-Ichi Kubo and Dr. Koichi Kawaguchi to come with you to the station? Thanks. Is there something else? I see. Well, what do you want me to do? Let the municipal boys deal with it. I wouldn't dream of interfering. Galan, if an old man blows his top outside the post office because he's been abandoned and tries to assault a municipal policeman who only wants to calm him down, it's nothing to do with us. We have things to do right now. Unless someone shoots someone else, we don't give a damn."

Sitting next to Fusco, in the same armchair (the same one as before, not the same one as Fusco), Massimo was looking down at the floor and waiting to start. Kawaguchi and Kubo had just arrived, with very different demeanors. Kawaguchi had sat down diligently to the right of Massimo and seemed much calmer than the previous time. Kubo, on the other hand, looked like someone who has slept little and badly, his eyes puffed with tiredness and his gestures nervous and uncoordinated. As soon as he had sat down, Fusco began.

"Before anything else, I apologize for summoning you again, but I need you to clarify a few aspects for us before you leave."

Having heard the translation, Kubo nodded.

"As you will recall, on the basis of certain testimonies, our investigations centered on Professor Asahara's laptop computer. Unfortunately, the contents of the laptop examined by us, which was indeed the professor's, did not live up to our expectations. There is however one aspect that did seem worthy of note. Translate, please."

More than translation was needed. Massimo freed Fusco's

remarks from the thick tangle of bureaucratic Italian and remolded them into acceptable colloquial English. After which, having heard the Japanese version, Kubo nodded for the second time.

"The aspect in question is the fact that a certain code was found in the Professor's computer. This code," Fusco went on, looking at Massimo with a conspiratorial air, "has been examined by our experts, who identified a number of peculiarities in it. Practically speaking, they found that a code programmed in that way could only have worked if run on computers equipped with an enormous memory. We have checked, and ascertained that the professor's computer was not equipped with the appropriate amount of memory. Unless, obviously, the same computer had been somehow tampered with."

Massimo translated, and while Koichi was translating, it seemed to Massimo that Kubo was turning slightly pale. This time he did not nod, but Fusco did not need any encouragement.

"At this point, Dr. Kubo," he continued, lowering his gaze to the surface of the desk, "I must ask you if you have a laptop computer."

Having heard the translation, Kubo nodded again and said something.

"He says yes, he has a laptop."

"Good. Dr. Kubo, I must ask you in my official capacity for permission to examine your laptop. In particular, I need to verify if the memory in your laptop is compatible with that of the laptop belonging to the late Professor Asahara, and possesses the characteristics required to run the code in question."

Massimo translated, and held his breath. They were at the crucial point. Massimo had no idea how Kubo might react. If Massimo's idea was wrong, he would probably burst out laughing. Or else he would look at them in polite Japanese surprise. Or maybe we'll never know, because as soon as Koichi had finished translating Dr. Kubo stood up, as white as a sheet. He looked Fusco in the eyes, and said a few well-articulated words.

Koichi translated, in a subdued voice. Massimo looked at Koichi, who nodded, and then looked at Fusco. He spoke in a tone that he hoped was neutral.

"He says he wants to make a statement."

Fusco looked at Massimo, and made a sign with his hand. There was no need to translate. Kubo began speaking in a determined voice, in short, concise sentences, at the end of each of which he looked at Koichi, who kept his gaze fixed on the floor. At the end, Koichi spoke.

As Koichi was speaking, Massimo felt two conflicting emotions.

On the one hand, there was a quiver of pride at the fact that he had been right. On the other, the awareness that the person in front of him, who was more or less the same age as him and didn't seem like a criminal in any way, was confessing to a murder. And it was he, Massimo, who had identified him, he who had taken the initiative, talked to Fusco, told him what, in his opinion, had happened, and suggested questioning Shin-Ichi Kubo.

And instead of making him feel proud, it made him feel bad. As if he had interfered in something that was no concern of his, a joke intended for a stranger, and had taken the victim aside and blurted everything out to him. Given the circumstances, and to shrug off the impression that he was somehow responsible for this whole mess, Massimo also now spoke in bureaucratic language.

"Dr. Kubo declares that he gave Professor Asahara a large dose of a benzodiazepine, and admits that in this way he caused his death. He maintains that at the moment he carried out this act he was unaware that the Professor suffered from myasthenia, and that he did not intend in any way to provoke death. Doctor Kubo's intention was to make Professor Asahara feel slightly ill, in order to distract his attention from the laptop computer in his possession, and in this way to steal its memory. The memory of the computer in question is of an experimental type, constructed using revolutionary technology and having more than sixty gigabytes at its disposal. This memory had been entrusted by the manufacturer to Professor Asahara as an expert in digital calculations, with the aim of testing its performance in calculating molecular simulations. Dr. Kubo stole it in order to hand it over to a technician from a competing company, which had promised Dr. Kubo a job as director of the calculations center in its Tokyo branch if he succeeded in handing over the memory."

The following morning, when Massimo entered the bar, he was confronted with a somewhat curious scene. Standing behind the counter, with the catalogue of an art exhibition open in front of her and the earphones of the Walkman in her ears, Tiziana was doubled over with laughter, while the old-timers watched her, highly pleased with themselves. It wasn't difficult to grasp what was going on: quite simply, the four of them were getting Tiziana to relive what they considered one of their most successful jokes. That is, the fake museum audio guide.

This trick had been performed regularly years before, in the course of those so-called excursions with the pots, whenever the excursion in question involved a visit to a museum. First, you bought in advance a catalogue of the museum to be visited, after which some particularly significant paintings were chosen, which were commented on by Aldo in his wonderfully musical voice on a normal audiocassette, of which several copies were then made. Each of these copies was put in a Walkman, which the old-timers distributed to the people taking part in the excursion, pretending that they were the official audio guides of the museum.

Obviously, the comments contained in the cassettes weren't exactly in keeping with the canons of art history and criticism. Massimo, for example, remembered in detail the commentary on the painting that Tiziana was looking at, a canvas by Rembrandt showing a fearsome-looking old lady in bonnet and ruff, which began thus:

"Rembrandt Harmenszoon van Rijn, *Portrait of My Mother-in-Law*. In this work, the master of Leiden effectively portrays his wife Geltrude's mother, Edelfriede Van Gunsteren, remembered by chroniclers of the period as one of the most terrifying ball-breakers in the whole of northern Europe. The woman, a housewife of humble origins, lived at her son-in-law's expense, sharing his house, criticizing his work and lifestyle from morning to night, and often complaining at mealtimes, while choosing the best morsels for herself, about the fact that her daughter had not married the rich tulip merchant Jacobsen. For his part, Rembrandt hated the woman and, in the presence of friends, invariably referred to her as 'a brothel cast-off'; but, since he dearly loved his wife, he was forced, when in her presence, to treat her with respect and, when she asked him, to paint her portrait. Rembrandt's real feelings emerge powerfully from the colors he chooses to depict the old bitch: of particular note is the chiaroscuro with which Rembrandt emphasizes her double chin and her greedy, calculating expression, befitting the madam of a fourth-rate brothel, a place to which the master hoped she would soon return."

While Tiziana continued laughing, the quartet greeted Massimo enthusiastically.

"All hail Miss Marple!" said Del Tacca, getting up out of his chair, which was quite unusual for him.

"Welcome back, son," Ampelio said with a smile. "We've been waiting for you."

I can imagine what you've been waiting for, Massimo thought. The newspaper lay on the table, open at the crime pages, which carried an account of how, the previous day, in the course of a police interview, Dr. Shin-Ichi Kubo, thirty-four years old, had confessed to being responsible for the death of Professor Asahara.

Once again, Massimo found himself thinking that there was something unnatural in the speed with which the results of the investigation, however partial, managed to cover the distance between the police station and the newspaper offices. The conclusion that Massimo had drawn was that the diligent Officer Galan, with his seminarian's air, was a little too fond of using the wrong confessional.

Massimo, for his part, had absolutely no desire to speak about the case. The sense of guilt he had felt the day before had kept him company all night long. It had been a terrible night in fact, and he had the sensation that he had not closed his eyes once. Stupid, I know, but there it is, and it isn't going to be easy to get rid of it.

The old-timers, on the other hand, were already in their positions, bristling with curiosity. As Massimo went behind the counter, Aldo piped up:

"Massimo, there's one thing I'm curious about."

"Of course," Massimo said. "You want to know when they're going to pay us for catering the conference. Unfortunately, I haven't phoned the Ricciardi woman yet."

"I don't give a damn about the Ricciardi woman," Aldo said. "What I'd like to know is if what's written in the newspaper is completely true."

"Usually no. However, in this case, yes. That fellow Shin-Ichi Kubo admitted killing his chief. Involuntarily, it seems. His intention was to make him sick by giving him a few Tavor pills. Unfortunately, he didn't know his chief had that illness, myasthenia. That's why what happened happened."

"And that's also written in the newspaper," Aldo replied. "But what I don't understand is what exactly the man wanted to do."

Massimo took a deep breath, resisting the temptation to tell Aldo to go to hell. For a moment, he thought about how he could explain to the group of old codgers that he didn't want to talk about the case because it upset him. On the other hand, there was also his personal pride, the awareness that he'd had

158 · MARCO MALVALDI

a good intuition (which was only to be expected) and a certain degree of courage (which was surprising). After a brief battle, the sense of guilt withdrew to a corner and the pride took center stage.

"All right, let's start from the beginning. What's the purpose of a computer? Grandpa, it's a rhetorical question. If you try to interrupt, I'll put poison in your grappa."

Ampelio closed his mouth.

"A computer is for counting. That's its purpose. Counting. Computer means calculator. All the other things you can do with a computer—write emails, watch porn movies, go on the Internet to download porn movies, and so on—are offshoots of that basic ability. Having said that, though, it's clear that the purpose for which an object exists is dictated by the way in which we use it. And a portable computer like a laptop is basically a means of communication. Surfing the Internet, making presentations, writing reports or novels, all while you're away from home."

Massimo sat down on a chair, but got up again almost immediately. To make this kind of speech, he needed to move about. To walk, to gesticulate, to do whatever, but to move. Meanwhile, Tiziana had closed the catalogue and taken the earphones out of her ears.

"When I spoke with Fusco two days ago, he told me that none of the programs you need to do these things were on that computer. Which means that for all practical purposes, it was useless. And, from the usual point of view, he was right. But from a general point of view, no. The computer could be used to perform its primary role. In other words, count."

The old-timers nodded.

"So: Professor Asahara's laptop could be used for counting. And it had one peculiarity: a brand-new kind of memory. A memory with a much larger capacity than those in common use. That was what Asahara was referring to, surely, when he said, more or less as a joke, that there was something in his computer that would destroy Watanabe. For some kinds of calculation like those that Watanabe makes, that memory would have a revolutionary impact. Everything clear so far?"

"No," Pilade said. "I don't understand why the memory is so important."

"It's a matter of time," Massimo explained. "The calculations we're talking about can take weeks, or even months. If you could do the same calculation in one day, you could do a lot more things. You'd have an advantage. That's why lots of people are doing research into how to speed up these calculations. There are two ways: the first is to make the algorithm quicker, the procedure you use to do things. The second is to try to build a faster machine. Watanabe belonged to the first school. I'm no expert, but from what I've been able to understand, this memory would speed up calculations to such an extent as to make Watanabe's work practically useless. All clear now?"

The old-timers' heads waved up and down. Massimo, who had continued to walk around the bar, stopped.

"In any case, the computers were involved, but Watanabe wasn't. And while we were trying to figure out what role the computers played in the case, we made a massive error. We took something for granted. Do you know the difference between a man of letters, a physicist, and a mathematician?"

"Is it that when mathematicians tell a story they're boring as hell?" Aldo ventured.

"So are physicists. Quite a few men of letters too, for that matter. No, it's an old joke. A man of letters, a physicist, and a mathematician are traveling through Scotland by train, and at a certain point they see a red sheep in a meadow. The man of letters looks at it and says, 'Interesting. In Scotland the sheep are red.' The physicist shakes his head and replies, 'No. In Scotland some of the sheep are red.' The mathematician gives them a pitying look and concludes, 'There's at least one meadow in Scotland, and there's a sheep at least one side of which is red.' It's a joke, but the idea is that, from a mathematician's point of view it's wrong to take anything for granted that you don't know for certain, just because it seems perfectly plausible and in line with what you've seen before. In this case, that sheep are all of one color. It's plausible, I don't have any evidence, but it's the likeliest thing, and so it's true. In life, we often reason like that. In mathematics, or generally in an investigation of any kind, that type of argument should be avoided."

Massimo stopped for a moment to catch his breath. God, I'm really in bad shape. I get out of breath just walking around the bar. From tomorrow I'm going to the swimming pool every day, and no buts about it. I'm thirty-seven years old, I look more like forty-five, and there are days when I feel like eighty-six.

He took a deep breath and continued:

"But that's exactly the mistake we made. We took it for granted that what was in the computer was something written, a document, whatever, and not something that was physically inside the computer. It's a bit like three-card monte: we were looking in the right direction, but we were concentrating on the detail we assumed was important, that is, the information content of the computer, and in doing that we neglected the context. The thing that allowed everything to work. In this case, the computer itself."

Massimo went to the far end of the bar, stood in front of the glass door, and looked outside.

"The computer itself," he repeated, "even though it didn't work and was completely unusable. But why didn't it work? And above all, had it ever worked? This is where I was an idiot. I knew perfectly well that, when Asahara arrived in Italy, the computer was still working. I knew it because, when Carlo opened the first file, at the University, he read aloud when it had been opened and modified the last time. Sunday, May 20, at 11 P.M. In other words, when Asahara was in his room at the Santa Bona, presumably busy giving a last polish to his beloved poems before going to bed and falling asleep in a horizontal position for a change."

Massimo turned, took his hands out of his pockets, and walked behind the counter.

"To sum up, we have a computer that can presumably be used for counting, that works on Sunday night, and doesn't work anymore on Tuesday morning. What changed between Sunday night and Tuesday morning? One simple thing, which could easily be taken out and put back in again. In other words, the memory."

Massimo came out from behind the counter and stood in front, leaning his hands on it.

"Basically," he continued, "the company that developed that memory gave it to Asahara so that he could test its performance on calculations of molecular dynamics. That was what the simple program on the laptop, simple but with a huge memory, was for. And thinking about it, here too I was an idiot not to understand immediately. Simple programs are generally used as tests, to see if everything is working. Kubo had been contacted by another company, which wanted to get its hands on that memory, to see if they were able to figure out its technology. That was why they promised him they'd hire him and give him a fabulous position if he could find a way to get that memory to them."

"You mean, instead of giving him money, they bribed this guy by telling him they'd give him a job?" Ampelio said. "Strange people, the Japanese."

"That depends on how you look at it. But forget about that for now. At this point, Kubo had the idea of giving Asahara the Tavor to make him feel a little sick. Nothing serious, just a little queasiness, enough to persuade him to go and lie down and have himself seen to by a doctor, or at any rate to distract him for half an hour. When Asahara was taken to Emergency, Kubo grabbed the opportunity to get his hands on the computer. But taking the whole computer was a risk. Apart from anything else, a laptop had been stolen that same day, and Kubo didn't want to be seen walking around with a laptop that wasn't his. But in a computer, even in a laptop, there are some parts that can very easily be taken out and put back again. And the memory is one of them. That's why Kubo had the brilliant idea of taking the memory from Asahara's computer and swapping it for the one in his own. In that way, though, neither of the two computers were able to work, because he'd put in a type of memory incompatible with the machine."

Pause. Massimo went and poured a little iced tea from the carafe, and took a hurried sip.

"And that's what screwed things up for him. The other day, when I went to the Internet café, I saw Kubo using one of the computers. That struck me as strange, because I knew Kubo had a laptop of his own. He said that in the course of his first interview. And I knew there was an Internet connection at the Santa Bona. So if you have a computer and the place where you're staying has a network, why go to an Internet café to read your mail? There can only be one answer: because your computer doesn't work. And the strange thing is, this is the second computer that doesn't work. Both computers belong to two Japanese, what's more, two Japanese who know each other. The first computer was still working on Sunday, when its owner arrived in Italy. And so was the second one, by its owner's own admission."

Pause, another sip.

"At this point, I had no idea what it all meant, but it struck me as a bit unlikely as a coincidence. That's why I started to think and something came into my mind. What came into my mind was that Kubo had said he'd never seen Asahara's laptop, whereas his other colleagues had recognized it. That also struck me as unlikely, thinking about it. This was where Kubo tried to play three-card monte: saying this wasn't Asahara's computer, and knowing what was inside, he was trying to make us think that there was another computer in circulation. Among other things, when Snijders phoned the secretary to find out what computer Asahara had done his presentation on, we were told that he had used a computer with Windows. In other words, a different computer than the one we'd found. It never occurred to us that Asahara might have gotten Kubo to prepare the presentation, as professors often do, on Kubo's own laptop, which used Windows."

Pause. Thinking again about the fact that he had stopped in the middle of the road, while the cars were passing, Massimo had a kind of shudder. He dismissed it and went on.

"Anyway, as I was thinking, Grandpa phoned me, because I'd forgotten to take him to the post office."

"That's not the only thing you forgot," Ampelio muttered.

"We'll talk about that later. As I was speaking on the phone, Grandpa used the word 'memory.' That was what made me think that Kubo's computer couldn't work because someone had changed the memory, and that the whole business of the computers might revolve around memory."

Pause, to make sure they were all following him. Apparently they were, so he went on.

"In addition, there was a simple program in Asahara's computer, and a simple program usually has two purposes: it can be used for educational purposes, that's true, but as I said before it can also be used as a test to check the computer's performance. So I phoned Carlo and asked him to do a test. What I was hoping was that the program wouldn't work, and that it wouldn't work for a particular reason. That he would tell me what was so special about Asahara's computer that would make the program work. When Carlo told me that the program wasn't working because it required too much memory, I realized I was right."

Pause, sip. And now I'm going to light a cigarette. The first one this morning, as it happens. Since everyone and his mother smokes in here these days, for once I'm going to smoke too. Massimo picked up the lighter and after lighting the cigarette continued:

"Changing a memory is simple, it takes ten seconds. Even a child could do it. At this point I took a chance. I went to Fusco, and told him what I thought had happened. The rest you know. When Fusco brought in Kubo, and asked him a specific question about the memory, Kubo realized he'd lost, and gave himself up. Without protesting, and without making a drama out of it."

And that really impressed me, Massimo thought. You have no idea how much.

No point in denying it, Massimo had felt a kind of admiration for Kubo, who, clearly with his back to the wall, had obeyed his sense of discipline and admitted his guilt. Massimo, like all of us, lived in a world that had long accustomed him to guilty people invariably professing their innocence. They used every tactic, from justifying their act as not being criminal to obstinately denying the evidence. Behavior like Kubo's, a person giving himself up and assuming full responsibility, even when what he had done went well beyond his intentions, was something he had not expected. He was almost certain that the image of Kubo, who had showed more dignity and self-confidence in confessing than in waiting, would not abandon him for quite a while.

"Anyway, that's it. Culprit found, crime admitted, all over. Now I don't want to hear any more about this business."

"All right, but from tomorrow," Del Tacca said, looking outside. "Because today, it seems to me you're going to have to tell the story all over again."

Following the direction of Pilade's gaze, Massimo turned. Outside the glass door, A. C. J. Snijders had just parked his bicycle, and, with a smile on his face, was heading calmly toward the bar.

Pisa, April 9, 2008

To End

This book would have stayed in limbo if it hadn't been for the help of a number of people.

I thank Walter and Francesca Forli for their help with medical matters (purely theoretically, that is: Walter is a neurosurgeon and, thank God, I haven't yet needed to be treated by him). For the same reason, I thank Laura Caponi, who complemented the Forlis' suggestions and read the manuscript with enormous care, correcting several errors and suggesting a few improvements.

I thank Virgilio, Serena, Mimmo, Letizia, Christian, my father and mother, and all those who read this book when it was still just a draft.

Above all, I thank Samantha. Firstly, for giving me the main idea for the story and helping me to refine it. Secondly, for reading and rereading these pages ad nauseam, and improving them considerably. Last but not least, for putting up with me while I was writing it, which I think was by far the hardest task.

Finally, I should like to give credit to two people who gave me the initial idea for two of the characters. Ampelio is a fairly faithful portrait of my grandfather Varisello, who spent ninety-three years commenting on everything he didn't like about the world (and that included a lot). Last but not least, in 1992 I met a barman who isn't totally ignorant of mathematics, and who shares with Massimo not only a name but also a particular way of treating his customers. If you go to Pineta and have a coffee in one of the bars in the center of town, you're quite likely to run into him.

ABOUT THE AUTHOR

Marco Malvaldi was born in Pisa in 1974.
Three-Card Monte is the second in the Bar
Lume series, featuring Massimo the Barman
and the four elderly sleuths. He is the win-
ner of both the Isola d'Elba Award and the
Castiglioncello Prize for his crime novels.